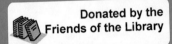

hunter's heart

hunter's heart

julia green

Carolrhoda Books, Inc. Minneapolis · New York

First American edition published in 2007 by Carolrhoda Books, Inc.
Originally published in Great Britain by Penguin Books Ltd.

Carolrhoda Books, Inc.
A division of Lerner Publishing Group
241 First Avenue North
Minneapolis, MN 55401 U.S.A.

Website address: www.lernerbooks.com

Library of Congress Cataloging-in-Publication Data

Green, Julia.
    Hunter's heart / by Julia Green. — 1st American ed.
      p. cm.
    Summary: During a long summer in the Cornish countryside, fourteen-
year-old Simon escapes his young sister and widowed mother, who is dating
his teacher, by indulging his obsessions with hunting, weapons, and an
attractive neighbor, a girl two years older and facing major problems of her
own.
     ISBN-13: 978-0-7613-9493-8 (lib. bdg. : alk. paper)
     1. Interpersonal relations—Fiction. 2. Family problems—Fiction.
3. Hunting—Fiction. 4. Single-parent families—Fiction. 5. Cornwall
(England : County)—Fiction. 6. England—Fiction.] I. Title.
PZ7.G82352Hun 2007
[Fic]—dc22   2006030224

Manufactured in the United States of America
1 2 3 4 5 6 – BP – 12 11 10 09 08 07

For Jim, with love

1

Thwack!

The stone from Simon's slingshot hits the rabbit between its ears. Perfect aim!

He crouches back on his heels, heart thudding. At last! He's done it! But there's something wrong. Why hasn't it just keeled over, dead? He watches, horrified, as the rabbit starts to twitch and jerk its body around and scream: a high, shrill squeal like a stuck pig might make. The noise is a shock. Rabbits are silent, aren't they? Pet ones in hutches, they never make a sound, however miserable they are, noses pushed up against the wire mesh. He's never heard a sound like this. You must be able to hear it for miles.

This rabbit is badly hurt, but not badly enough. It's writhing in agony, and Simon knows he's going to have to do it: go up close and kill it properly. He looks about for a heavy stick, or a rock or something, but the field is perfectly bare—a hayfield, recently mown.

He glances over his shoulder, as if someone might be there suddenly. Someone who could take over. It's not that he doesn't know what to do—he's read it often enough in the survival handbook: *The way to dispatch a rabbit hu-*

manely and certainly. It's just that it's different now, here. For real. And of course there isn't anyone around to help. No one for miles. Just him and the wounded rabbit on the grass.

He could run home, the sound of the rabbit's cry ringing in his ears. A fox would find it soon enough, wouldn't it? With that racket.

The rabbit's looking at him. Dark pained eyes boring into his own. Why won't it die? He takes a step forward, crouches over the rabbit, reaches out his hand. The terrified animal trembles violently, tries to run, can't. Simon grabs it, one hand round its neck, the other round the hind legs. *A smart, firm, stretching action*. He breaks its neck. Feels it crunch.

Now the rabbit is silent, limp, a small grey brown strip of fur, unbearably soft. Its eyes have glazed over. His throat tightens, aches. *No, not here, not now. Ridiculous to feel like this*. Dry sobs rise in Simon's throat but he won't let them out, even though no one is watching, no one could possibly know. He swallows and swallows until they've gone.

He's killed his first rabbit. He's a hunter, a survivor. He picks it up by its feet and starts to walk back across the hayfield to the stile and the lane. It feels so light, swinging as he walks, the soft fur brushing the bare skin of his leg. He starts to shape the story in his mind, the story of the day he caught his first rabbit, ready to tell to Johnny and Pike and Dan.

Friday, July 10th.

He won't forget this day.

He doesn't know it now, but later he'll look back and realize that this was how it all started. The death of the rabbit was the first thing. It marked the beginning of a summer that changed everything.

It's one thing telling his friends. It'll be different at home. He braces himself as he pushes open the back door.

"Hi, Mum. I'm back!" he calls out.

"Good," she calls. "Supper's almost ready. Ellie's been asking for you; it's her bedtime. Go up, will you?"

Simon dumps the bag on the pantry floor, lays the dead rabbit carefully on the draining board, washes his hands unasked. Then he thuds upstairs.

Ellie's calling him. He stands in the doorway to her room. She's sitting in bed, in stupid spotty dalmatian pajamas, sucking her thumb. Ellie's only six.

She's in tears.

"What?" he asks her, irritated.

"I saw," Ellie sobs. "In your hand. When you were coming up the yard."

"What?"

"The baby rabbit," Ellie wails. "How could you do that?"

"It's just the same as the meat you eat," Simon says. "You eat chicken, don't you? And sausages? What's the difference?"

"It *is* different, it *is*. It's *not* the same. You are so horrible. I hate you!"

Simon pulls a face. He turns to go downstairs.

"Get Mum. I want her to come and tuck me in," Ellie whines after him.

He clatters noisily down the bare wooden stairs. They haven't gotten a carpet yet. He waits in the pantry until he's heard Mum go up to Ellie. He scoops up the rabbit and takes it into the kitchen. Now he needs the survival book, to check what you do next.

Mum reappears. She stands in the doorway, staring at him.

"I didn't think I'd hit it, but when I did I thought it was better to bring it home and eat it." He doesn't look at her directly. The small furry animal is now lying on the kitchen table, too near the salad.

"You deal with it, then," she hisses between clenched teeth, "while I sort out Ellie."

What's all the fuss about? She knows about the slingshot; he showed it to her in the catalogue before he sent off the money, and she didn't stop him. She's already said no to the BB gun, and the crossbow, and the air rifle.

It isn't fair. No one else has a mother like her. Or if they do, they have a father to water it down. Mostly, the dads like the idea of air rifles and slingshots. Johnny's does, anyway. He had stuff like that when he was a kid. He knows how to make arrowheads and all sorts of things. Johnny's dad has an air rifle of his own and sometimes he lets them have a turn when they go over there after school.

Still, he wore her down with arguing eventually, and she said he could have the slingshot if he paid for it with his own money, but he must never *ever* aim it at a person blah blah blah. He hadn't listened to the rest. And he didn't tell her what the slingshot could do. It's made of stainless steel and rubber and leather. With a large enough stone as shot and perfect aim, you could kill a person.

For a moment, Simon catches the image of the rabbit again, twitching and jerking about in agony, and he pushes and pulls the picture till it becomes a person, a sort of soldier, covered in blood and mud and aiming a gun at Simon's head so he has to shoot in self-defense. . . .

The rabbit's fur is so soft. The way it's lying on the table, it could just be sleeping. It's not very big, hardly enough for a meal for one. Just a baby, really.

He could bundle the whole thing into a plastic bag and drop it in the trash. He hates the way she just gives him that look, without saying anything. But he really wants to see the whole thing through. If you don't eat it, then there's no point. You're just some sort of evil person, killing stuff for no reason. Like the boys down at the park, biking over frogs and laughing when their insides spurt out. That's just sick.

Simon pushes the salad bowl to one side and leans *The SAS Survival Guide* up against it, turned to the page about skinning and jointing a rabbit. If he does it step by step, like a sort of operation, just looking at one bit at a time, he can stop himself thinking about it being a baby rabbit. The first cut is the worst.

Once the skin's finally off, it's just a lump of meat. Pale pink. He puts it in a glass casserole dish in the oven to cook. It looks too small, so he takes it out again and adds some onions and a carrot, a sprinkle of basil leaves from the pot on the windowsill and some water. He likes cooking because it's science, really. When they did a survey way back in elementary school, about sixty per cent of the boys said they wanted to be chefs when they grew up. The teacher said it was because of Jamie Oliver and all those other TV celebrity chefs. The real reason was, they'd all copied Rick Singleton, the richest, coolest kid in class, who'd only written it down for a laugh.

That's one of the good things about moving to this new house: it's much further away from Rick Singleton's house. Rick goes to a different middle school now too; a private one. It's a relief not having to watch over your shoulder on the walk home in case Rick's lurking behind a wall ready to get you. He gets you with words, not fists or stones or broken glass. The words, though, are sharp enough to tear you up inside. He's got it in for Simon for some reason. Or maybe no reason.

Sometimes, his new slingshot in his pocket, Simon still thinks about Rick Singleton in his navy blue uniform with a crest on the blazer pocket.

Simon hears his mother's footsteps padding downstairs. She stands for a moment in the doorway, surveying the scene. *What's she thinking?*

"Clear that mess off the table. Now. Supper will be ruined."

Upset *and* angry, then.

Simon puts the knives and the chopping board into the sink, wipes the table with the towel on the draining board, rinses it halfheartedly.

She won't come into the kitchen until it's all completely cleared away.

"And open the window. The smell makes me feel sick."

He can tell she's almost ready to cry, but he won't let it get to him. He hums the theme music from *The Great Escape* under his breath, just to show her how relaxed and happy he is. It's just natural, catching your own food. It's total hypocrisy, eating meat and making such a fuss about the killing of it. Even if the fuss is a silent one.

She's looking at him as if he's a stranger. Not her son. She keeps telling him how different he is these days. *Sometimes when you're upstairs talking to Ellie, I think for a moment there's a strange man up there.*

And it's not just his voice.

Fourteen! You're growing up, Si. You're almost taller than me.

"Pasta and sauce?" she asks him once she's back in the kitchen. She's thrown the towel in the trash, run boiling water over the bloodied knife.

"Nah. I'll wait for the rabbit to cook."

"As you like."

He's vaguely aware of her serving herself a small bowl, hardly eating anything.

"Ellie cried and cried," she says, as if it's all his fault.

Why does she have to go on? It's what she always does. As if crying about things makes you morally right or something. He goes out of the kitchen, turns the television on in the front room. Friday night. Comedy night. He flips the channels. Fragments of news blast out into the quiet room:

". . . Warplanes, guided by special forces soldiers on the ground, began an intense bombardment. . . . pockets of strong resistance . . .

". . . A second suicide bomb exploded in a busy restaurant in the center of the city. . . .

". . . Aviation officials are considering the introduction of anti-missile protection for all planes. . . .

". . . A youth involved in a fatal crash was jailed today. . . ."

He flips channels again. There's a preview of some

Scottish stand-up comedian telling jokes about men and sex. He won't be watching that later, unless Mum's already in bed. It doesn't get dark till really late. It's partly because it's midsummer—well, July—and also because of being so far west. He read somewhere that real local time is twenty minutes later than Greenwich Mean Time.

He can hear owls outside in the trees. It's one of the things he likes about the house. He likes his room, too, and the yard, and the fact that although their road is at the edge the town, it's also really close to the fields. You are never more than about three miles from the sea wherever you are. It's almost like living on an island.

Mum goes to bed early. He eats the rabbit stew in front of the TV. It tastes good. Like chicken, but with more small bones. He watches one program after another, the comedian, and then a film, and by the time he drags himself up to bed his mind's just a fuzz, a blur.

Whooo. Whoooo. The owls again. They will be hunting over the yard, swooping silently over the fields. He goes to sleep thinking about the soft wings, and the sharp beak, and the claws.

2

He's slept in late. He can tell from the angle of the sun on the wall and the sounds from outside: cars, voices, people parking here for free and making their way down to the town or the beach, loaded with picnics and windscreens and surfboards. He lies with his arms behind his head, adjusting to the idea of being awake. His head's been full of weird dreams, of knives and blood, and hunting dogs with slavering jaws coming after him all night. And then he was somewhere dark and terrifying, deep underground, and he couldn't find the way out.

He blinks. The room is shockingly bright. They painted the walls blue, but there aren't any curtains yet. The first morning they were here, back in May, he was standing at the window in just his boxers and there was this girl in the house opposite standing at her window, staring right in. She's about sixteen. She's done her final exams, the GCSEs, already; hangs around all the time, doing nothing. Mum has her eye on her as a potential babysitter for Ellie. She's given up on him, thank goodness. It's just that he never knows whether he's going to be in or not. He doesn't plan ahead. And it's not fair, anyway. Why can't she just watch TV and put herself to bed?

He knows why, really. She's scared of the dark. She's only six.

Simon pulls on jeans and a T-shirt, keeping well back from the window. He ought to fix something up, a sheet or something, until Mum gets the curtains done. She says she's too busy at the moment; he'll have to wait till vacation. Only ten more days. They're not going anywhere this summer because of just moving. In any case, this is a vacation place itself. People come from all over. But everyone else will be going away, Johnny and Dan and Pike and— well, they're the only people who count, really, from school. They'll be going off with their families. Exciting places like the Picos de Europa (Johnny) and South of France (Dan). Pike will be sailing somewhere with his dad and his million brothers and sisters (well, five).

But they're planning to go off camping by themselves first, just the four of them: him, Johnny, Pike, Dan. He hasn't told Mum yet. *Nina*, not Mum. He's trying to remember to call her that. It doesn't sound so . . . so childish.

Without meaning to, Simon finds himself standing at the bare window. The girl's there, leaning against the gate. Her hair flops down over her face as she swings with one foot on the half-open gate. Fair hair, past her shoulders. She's wearing one of those short tops that shows off your stomach. As usual. You can't help noticing the smooth tanned flesh, the way it shadows towards the hip bone. Simon flushes, looks away.

Johnny, Dan, Pike, and him aren't interested in girls. That is, they never talk about them. And the girls in ninth grade (their grade) just ignore them. That's just how it is. For now.

Mum/Nina yells up the stairs. "Are you getting up at all today?"

Simon bangs open his door, stands at the top of the stairs, gives her his cool, calculated look.

"Been up for hours."

"Oh yes? Well, then, you can go into town for me and do some shopping. Take Ellie with you. And there's washing-up to do."

He spends a long time in the bathroom, mostly looking at his face in the mirror above the basin. Two zits. His hair looks weird.

Sunlight is flooding through the open back door. Ellie's sitting on the step, making something with glitter and stones and an old wine bottle, while Mum writes out a list of shopping.

"Look!" Ellie holds out her creation.

"What is it?" He tries not to sound sarcastic. Ellie looks at him, expecting something more enthusiastic.

He swings his backpack over one shoulder and picks up the list.

"Have some breakfast first," Nina says.

"Not hungry. Still full of rabbit stew."

Ellie looks up; should she cry or not? Not.

He studies the list. Nothing too embarrassing. But he's not taking Ellie.

"Please, Si. Then I can get on with things."

"No way. She can't walk fast enough. It takes too long. She moans all the way back up the hill."

Nina sighs.

He almost relents, but then he imagines what it will be like if he bumps into someone from school, and that does it.

"I'm going on my bike, anyway."

"Don't forget your helmet!" Nina yells after him as he disappears out to the shed.

Simon grins to himself. It's not that he deliberately upsets her, pretending he's reckless and foolhardy, but she does go on and on.

The girl from the house opposite watches him get on to his bike, fasten his helmet, freewheel down the hill.

The town's packed with shoppers, cars bumper to bumper in the narrow streets. Simon weaves in and out, bumps up onto the pavement for a bit, but it's even more congested. People stop suddenly and unexpectedly to look at things in windows or to talk to someone. *It's as if I'm invisible*, he thinks. *They just don't see me.* He ends up pushing the last bit, down the cobbled street that leads to the small supermarket where he can get most of the stuff. There's a girl he recognizes from school at one register, so he goes to the other.

He might as well go all the way down to the sea, since he's here. He swings the backpack back over one shoulder, heavy and lumpy with shopping now, and scoots through the series of narrow alleyways and cobbled streets that lead down to the town beach. Already, families are parked with windscreens and picnics all along the dry sand at the top near the wall. An ice-cream van is dealing out cheap whipped white stuff in cones. There's a line at the fish-and-chips stand, and a crowd of boys hanging round the front of the amusement arcade, hands in pockets, hair slicked up. One of them looks a bit like Rick Singleton. Simon gives them a wide berth, scoots farther along next to the sea wall, finds a place to lean the bike.

The sea's sparkling. No big surfing waves, just small ripples lapping onto the sand. Two dogs race in circles through puddles left by the retreating tide, even though this is a No-Dogs-May-to-October beach. They're chasing seagulls and barking, though the sound is whipped away by the wind. Offshore today. You have to be careful with an offshore wind. That's the one that whisks you out in your small inflatable: the child's dolphin boat or the small boy on a bodyboard, and before you know it you're way out of the bay. Every year there are drownings.

"Six people last season," the fish-shop man said as he wrapped their chips the first weekend after they moved. "And mostly strangers, tourists. They don't respect the sea. They think you can come here and do what you like, but she's a terrible one, she is. No mercy in her. There was a lad and his father down on the rocks, fishing, and the first wave came and washed the lad off, and the next one got the father. They didn't think, see."

Simon wanted to hear the whole story in detail. Nina hustled him out before he could ask about the other four deaths. "What's wrong with you? You're obsessed," she hissed at him.

You'd never imagine it, looking at that tame sea out there now. It's easier to believe if you walk up along the cliff path for a bit, the way it crashes in on the rocks at high tide. The water is way below the path, but the spray gets you even in summer. They arrived in May; it's July now.

There haven't been any big storms yet. He can't wait!

"Still soft in the head, eggbrain?" The words whisper into his skull from close range. A long shiver rattles his backbone.

"Thought you'd escaped, didn't you, Simple Simon?"

Simon doesn't need to turn round to see whose shadow it is that's fallen over his propped-up bike. He puts one hand on the handlebars to steady himself, waiting for what's coming next. But Rick's moving on, hands in pockets, swaggering after the bunch of lads sauntering down the pavement toward the boy who collects money for the deckchairs. Simon doesn't hang around. He shifts the backpack onto both shoulders, ready for the steep ride home. Sweat trickles down his neck.

He's red as a beetroot by the time he reaches his house. The girl across the road is still hanging out at the front of her house. She straightens up when she sees him, watches him dismount and wheel the bike to the shed. *I'm hot because of the bike ride*, he wants to explain. But he doesn't say a word, of course.

Simon humps the heavy bag on to the kitchen table. A sack of onions rolls out onto the floor, but he leaves them there. Ellie and Nina are nowhere to be seen. He thumps upstairs to the bathroom and pours cold water over his head. Most of it drips onto the floor. The sun has moved around; his room is in shadow now. He lies on the unmade bed for a while, waiting for his heart to stop pounding. He imagines himself swimming out into the bay, the feel of the waves slapping over his head.

Then he thinks of Rick, sauntering along the edge of the town beach. He can't swim there, can he? But there's another place. If he can remember how to get there. Some guy from one of the farms told Nina about it, when they were out walking: "I've swum there since I was a boy. You have to watch the tide. It's only safe at a low spring tide. You know, the extra low ones at full moon. We don't tell many people about it." He winked at Simon and his mother.

Simon checks his slingshot's safe in his pocket. He retrieves his knife from the kitchen windowsill. The blade's clean and shiny and sharp. He leaves the back door unlatched, like they do these days. Back at the old house, they always kept doors locked. Even windows. Since they've been here they've let all that go. No one locks doors round here.

The girl across the way has disappeared.

It's so hot the blacktop is melting. It sticks to his boots. The road's gone quiet, like it often does in the early afternoon on a summer Saturday. He turns left along a small shady lane towards the fields. From there he can cut across to the coast path.

The grass is stubbly and scratchy from where it's been cut. He watched them last week, cutting the hay and then binding it into rolls and trailering them behind the tractor, back to the farm. The field was covered in crows. He liked the feeling, as he watched, that it all belonged to him now. Not literally, but just because this is where he hangs out, now that they live so close. He's left behind the built-up town where they used to live. The traffic and the concrete, and all the crap: shops and parking lots and people crowded like rats into shopping malls and pedestrian walkways. He hates all that. Even the words are ugly.

When he's older, he's going to live somewhere really wild. Alone. He'll build himself a house in the middle of a forest or a wilderness of some kind and live off the land. Hunting, fishing. That sort of thing. He doesn't tell anyone this. Not even Dan or Johnny or Pike.

He can see the sea now, a wide blue expanse of the bay, as far as the lighthouse one way, and thinning to nothing the other. It feels like the edge of the world. The air changes as you get closer to the cliff. There are hundreds of gulls. He climbs over a gate on to the footpath and starts walking westwards.

3

It feels as if he's going to walk off the cliff edge into thin blue air. He can't see the narrow rough path zigzagging down the cliff until the very last minute. Someone's tied a rope to a wooden fence post and placed some old sacking over the barbed wire. You'd crack your head open on the rocks below if you fell.

But he's so hot, and the sea below is a beautiful turquoise. The tide's so far out he can see there'll be sand in the cove soon. It's perfect timing. He starts to climb down, one hand grasping the coarse fiber of the rope, the other steadying himself on the rock. He feels for footholds without looking down. Already there's more wind, the air's cooler.

The path takes him onto a platform of layered rock, with rock pools in the gaps. Simon can't resist; he lies down next to one of the pools so as not to cast a shadow and cups his hand round a small speckled fish, lets it squirm and tickle his palm before he releases it. The fish darts under a rock. The edges of the pool are studded with sea anemones.

This was as far as he came, that time before with Nina, but it's too hot today on the rocks; he's determined to swim.

He lowers himself down the other side of the spine of rock sticking out into the sea, dangles precariously, drops the last few feet onto another, flatter rock. He strips off his clothes; no one can see him. Then he jumps.

Ahhh! Simon gasps at the shock. The water's freezing! It's nothing like its Mediterranean color. He gulps air, ducks his head under, shakes his hair as he surfaces again, then swims fast, overarm strokes into the cove. He turns on to his back, floats, rests his head back into the water. The sun shines full on his face; he has to squeeze his eyes closed against the brightness. Where the water's shallow enough he puts a foot down onto wave-ridged sand. The water comes up to his armpits. If the tide goes down a bit further there might eventually be a sandy beach. But it's much too cold to keep still for long. He kicks out again, right across the cove and back to the rock. It's hard to get enough grip to pull himself out. The rock is slippery, sharp with barnacles. He hauls himself up and over and stands up, water streaming off his body.

He's trembling with cold, with the effort of swimming and pulling himself out. A thin trickle of blood seeps down one leg where he's snagged it. He struggles back into his clothes, the fabric sticking to his wet legs and torso, then he sits back for a minute. His whole body feels glowing now, truly alive, even though his teeth are chattering. He glances up at the cliff to check that no one has witnessed his naked swim, but of course there's no one there. Probably no one for miles.

Barefoot, he climbs back up to the flat platform and stretches out to warm himself in the sun. He dozes. His ears are full of the sound of hundreds of seabirds, swooping and diving and squabbling over the cliff face. There's the chug of a boat engine, and then a small ferryboat comes into view, taking tourists around the coast to see the seals. They might have thought he was one, had they been there only minutes earlier, his wet head sleek like the dark shape of a seal's.

Gradually he warms up. Several times he hears small showers of soil and stones trickling down the cliff side. He frowns slightly. *Must have loosened the rock with my feet when I was climbing down. Or perhaps it's a small animal, or a bird.* He watches for a while, slightly uneasy, but there's nothing there as far as he can see. *Unless there's someone right at the top of the path, out of view . . .*

After a while he stops thinking about it. He dozes in the sun and studies creatures in the rock pools and wonders which of the shellfish are edible. He'll have to look it up later. He starts overheating again, so he clambers down a level and dangles his feet in the sea, but he doesn't swim. The tide seems to be coming back up. No sandy beach ever appears. When he finally clambers back up the cliff and along the coast path for home his face is burning from too much sun and wind, but he feels amazing. He's thirsty. He finds a clump of wild strawberries at the edge of the footpath. Each tiny fruit bursts on his tongue with sweetness.

The girl is sitting on the front wall. She watches Simon as he trudges up the hill and when he's almost level with her she speaks.

"Hi."

Her voice jolts him out of a daze.

"Hi," he mumbles. It comes out wrong, a sort of grunt.

He bows his head lower, crosses the road, and dives into his own front yard.

"What the hell've you been doing, Simon?" Nina stands at the back door, hands on hips like a cartoon mother.

"Nothing. Just been for a walk."

"Where?" she asks, suspicious. "And couldn't you have left us a note?"

"*You* didn't. You weren't here when I got back from town."

"I was gone for a few minutes, that's all. I took Ellie down to her friend's. Anyway, what am I doing, justifying myself to you?"

"You don't usually mind. I only went over to the fields."

"Who with?"

"No one. Just me."

She scrutinizes his face. She always used to know when he was lying, when he was little. Not any more.

"Anything could happen, Simon."

"Like what?"

She glares at him. "I need to know where you are. You know I don't like you going off by yourself. It's different with friends. There's all sorts of dangers. Different ones, here. The sea, cliffs, mineshafts . . . you know."

Yes. You go on about it enough, he thinks. She even has the statistics. "*By the age of fifteen boys are three times more likely than girls to die, from accidents, violence, suicide. . . .*"

"Go and have a shower. Your face is red as anything. Didn't you take a hat? Sunscreen?"

Here we go. Doesn't she realize no one his age wears hats, or sunscreen for that matter? Get real, Nina. But he doesn't say anything. Just dumps his bag in the kitchen and runs himself a glass of cold water.

His mother follows him. In the darkness inside he can't see her properly. He shrinks back as he feels her reach out to touch his face.

"We were so close once, Si. You never used to mind telling me things."

Simon turns away, closes his eyes. "Leave it, Mum."

He can feel her watching him as he tramps upstairs. He goes into the bathroom, locks the door, sits on the closed lid of the toilet seat, head in his hands. If she'd guessed he'd been swimming in the sea by himself at that cliff place, she'd have gone nuts. She lives in terror of something happening to him or Ellie, as if his father's awful accident has somehow made it more likely that something will happen again.

He doesn't really remember much about it. His clearest memory is of Ellie, a tiny baby then, crying in the night, on and on, sounding more and more desperate, and Mum still not coming. He knew then that something was up. He had to get out of bed and go into his parents' room, and there the baby was, bawling her eyes out, but his parents' bed was empty, the covers half pushed back. He stroked Ellie's little back and said things, and when she quieted down a bit and started sucking her fist he could hear noises from downstairs. Low voices, and a weird sobbing noise like an animal.

His dad died in a motorcycle accident. Ran off the road; no one could work out why or how. "I never wanted him to have the bloody bike in the first place," Nina tried to explain much later, "but he clung onto it. It reminded him of being younger and freer. That's what I think, anyway. He *liked* the risk. But then . . ." She had started to cry, even though it was years later.

Simon doesn't often think about it, but lately he's started up again, for some reason. Maybe because of what Nina has started saying. "You're getting so like him, you know. Sometimes it gives me such a shock. I think it's him standing in the shadows."

He can't help what he looks like. Can't stop himself from growing up, can he?

Leah has spent all afternoon in her yard, turning herself around as the sun moves across the sky, like a spit-roast pig. She's turning a beautiful shade of golden brown all over. She started during the warm-up to the GCSEs; all that extra time off for studying, and the weather was gorgeous. Her hair's gone lighter too; gold highlights for free: you'd pay thirty pounds at the salon. ("Naughty 'n' Nice"—stupid name. What's naughty about having a haircut?) Two girls from her old tutor group have Saturday jobs there, sweeping up and doing shampoos, but the money's terrible. You won't catch Leah working her socks off for that sort of rubbish. She's got more sense. She's been looking around for something interesting to do, something that pays more than the minimum wage. She hasn't found it yet, but in the meantime it's just fine lying in the yard all day, perfecting her tan, with the radio on to drown out the arguments from indoors. Her mother's "not well" again, and getting worse. They never talk about it. Dad's mostly out. They won't be going on vacation like everyone else from school. It's been so long since they did anything together that she hardly notices anymore. And she can't invite anyone over, not with her mother in such a state. The girls in her class stopped bothering with her years ago. It's easier like that, really. Not having to think up excuses all the time.

The new boy across the road looks cute. Too young for her, of course, but it's fun to make him squirm. His mother's called Mrs. Piper but there doesn't seem to be a Mr. Piper around. She's probably a single mom, one of those women who have children on their own and think men are redundant these days. Leah knows differently.

Since the Piper family moved in (May 21st—she wrote it in her diary), they have painted the front door and had the old carpets taken away and tidied up the yard. They still haven't put up curtains in the front bedroom. You can see right in when the light's on at night. It's the boy's room. It's got blue walls and stuff hanging from the ceiling—like model airplanes and other kids' things. There's a wooden boat propped up on the window frame, its sail filling one half of the glass. Perhaps he thinks it stops from her seeing in.

They've all got bikes, even the little girl. It's too hilly for bikes around here, they'll soon find out. The boy goes off on his own a lot. Doesn't hang out with the soccer gang down at the park, or the surfing crowd at the town beach.

Where does he go?

Leah opens her eyes. The late afternoon sun is still hot enough to burn. She carefully oils her shoulders, tucks in the straps of her top so she won't get white lines. Sometimes she wonders why she bothers: who's to see? Who cares? But there's somebody out there who's just about to. She can sense it: he's out there, somewhere, and moving closer. It won't be long now. She closes her eyes. He'll have dark hair and blue eyes, and hands with sensitive fingers. She'll know him when she sees him. The warm sun on her arms spreads through her body. That's what it will be like when he touches her for the first time.

For the last half hour Simon has been lying upstairs on his bed reading the survival guide. "Chapter Four: Living from the Land." It's made him hungry. He picks up the book, takes it with him down to the kitchen, opens the fridge and scans the contents. He takes three slices of salami, a hunk of Cheddar cheese, and a slab of fruit-and-nut chocolate. He leans against the backdoor frame. Nina is sitting in a deckchair under the tree, reading a book. He watches her for a while. It's unusually quiet without Ellie around.

"Did you know," Simon says, "that there is no known antidote to eating a deadly fungus? The most deadly are the *Amanita* genus."

"Mmm." She's obviously not really listening. She turns the page of her book.

Simon carries on regardless. He reads aloud about the Fly Agaric (*Amanita muscaria*) through Destroying Angel (*Amanita virosa*) to Death Cap (*Amanita phalloides*), the most deadly fungus known.

Nina stops reading and looks at him. He's got her attention now, but she evidently hasn't heard a word he's said.

"You look lovely," she tells him. "Your hair like that. With the sun on it."

He rolls his eyes, but there's no stopping her in midflow. "When you were a little boy, people used to stop me in the street to say how lovely you were! 'He'll break a few hearts, won't he, with eyes like those,' they'd go, and I'd smile and nod, and say, 'He's got his father's eyes, actually.' You do, Si. You're even more like Jason now."

Simon doesn't want to think about all that again. He carries on reading out bits from his book instead. "Many fungi are useful for medicine, food, or other purposes, such as dyeing and fire lighting. Edible fungi often have very similar poisonous cousins," he reads aloud, "so care in identification is essential."

She's listening properly now.

"I don't want you picking fungi, Simon," she says. "It's too risky."

"It's not, if you know what you're doing," Simon says with relish. "That's why I'm reading this. For when we go camping. We're going to hunt and collect all our food and cook it. You can live off the land completely, you know." He looks at her defiantly, waiting for her to react.

"I absolutely forbid it, Simon! No fungi. You know how dangerous they can be! And that's my last word on the matter. Subject closed."

Simon smiles. It's so easy to get her going.

He gets his knife out of his pocket and starts carving his initials in the bark of the plum tree. She hates that. She picks up her book again and settles herself back in the deckchair without speaking.

Simon kicks the tree trunk and an unripe plum plops onto the grass. Nina frowns.

He walks through the yard away from the house to the bit they still haven't cleared. It's full of brambles and bindweed with huge white flowers like trumpets. Tight red berries are already forming on the brambles. He started making a den in there when they first arrived, but Ellie wanted to join in and turn it into a playhouse, so he gave up. If only he had a brother. He could have asked Johnny, maybe, but he's pretty sure it's not OK to make bramble dens when you're fourteen (almost definitely not) and he can't risk it. For some reason that makes him think about Rick Singleton again, and he shivers. What was Rick doing there in the town? Supposing he's around all summer? Finds out where Simon lives?

His mother's voice drifts over. "Going to fetch Ellie. Won't be long."

He doesn't reply. When she's gone, he gets his slingshot from the bag he left in the old kitchen, fishes a handful of stones from his pocket, does target practice on the fence at the bottom of the garden. He's getting better: almost one hundred per cent accuracy now. As soon as he's saved up enough he's going to get an air rifle. He's chosen the model, seen it in the magazine he borrowed from Pike. He's looked up on the Internet about the law too. And trespassing, and poaching, and the Wildlife and Countryside Act. He's thorough like that. Then he can hunt properly. Rabbits, pheasants, that sort of thing.

That girl's still watching him. She's always there. She's standing a bit farther along the pavement, next to the hedge, trying to see what the noise is: small stones hitting wood at close range. Simon flushes. He puts the slingshot away again before his mother gets back. She doesn't like him to use it with Ellie around.

He goes back inside to wait for something, anything, to happen. On his table there's a jumble of schoolbooks and old gym clothes, untouched. The thought of having to do homework fills him with despair. Perhaps he won't bother. It's nearly the end of the term, isn't it? It's not as if it does any good. He hates school, everything except art and sometimes geography, when it's about interesting places, like the Skeleton Coast. Or Canada. He likes to read about how people used to live, too. Like hunter-gatherers, tribal people, people who knew about the land. But you don't do that in school.

Ellie bounces upstairs.

"Hello, Simon. Look what I've got—"

"Go away."

Her face crumples.

He knows he's being mean, but he can't help it. Something about how joyful she is, how *unencumbered*, brings out the worst in him.

In her hand she's holding four little figurines. She lets her hand droop.

"What are *they*?"

Immediately she brightens again, oblivious to the sneer in his voice.

"They're for my dollhouse. A new family. They're the same as Amy's. Her mummy got them for me."

Nina calls up the stairs. "Get your schoolwork done tonight, Si, and then we can have a day out all together to-morrow. I'm cooking supper now."

Simon lies on his bed, legs crossed, head resting on his interlaced hands, eyes shut. Ellie's still chatting away to her miniature family, putting them in the dollhouse, making them do things. She counts them out: Mummy, Daddy, big girl, baby. She's written him out, then. No room in the dollhouse for a mean older brother.

It's half past eight. In the house opposite, Leah sits at the dressing table in her room, peering at herself in the dusty mirror as she strokes black eyeliner along her lids. Her eyes look huge. She pulls down her top slightly to see the white line of flesh which shows her how brown she is now. She wishes there was a place she could sunbathe with nothing on. Then she could be that color all over. The light is on the boy's room across the road. She goes and stands at the window. After only a few minutes, the boy comes over to his, as if he knows she is there, as if he's been pulled by some mysterious, invisible thread. It is this same irresistible magnetism which will pull her true lover to her, Leah believes. She only has to wait. For now, she's just practicing her powers. She lifts her hand and beckons to the boy to come down, outside. She walks downstairs and out to the path to meet him. Now she just has to decide what she's going to say.

Did he imagine it? She sort of waved, didn't she? And acted like she wanted to speak to him. Simon's heart thuds.

He must have imagined it. Why would she want to speak to him? He knows his face is red again: part sunburn, part—mostly—embarrassment. He runs his hands through his hair. Finds himself walking downstairs and out into the yard.

She's leaning over her gate, her hair falling softly onto her tanned, smooth shoulders. She smiles.

"Come here a minute, you," she says in this confusing

way. "What's your name?"

She talks as if he's a small child. But, then, that's exactly what he feels like at this precise minute.

"Si-Simon." He stammers.

"I thought you should know, Simon, that when the light's on people can see right into your room." She still smiles.

"So?" He shrugs, as if he doesn't care. Inside, he's curling up with something he can't name.

"So get some curtains, Simon!"

He turns away, walks back across the road.

She calls softly after him. "Just some friendly advice, that's all."

He's hot round his neck and up to his ears. Burning.

"Don't you want to know my name, then? Since we're neighbors?"

He hesitates.

That soft voice at his back, almost a whisper.

"It's Leah. Leah Sweet."

Is she pulling his leg, or what? *Sweet?* Can that be a surname?

"Pleased to meet you, Simon Piper."

How does she know that? Simon makes a run for the back door and almost collides with his mother, who is carrying a colander of vegetable peelings out to the compost heap.

"Whoops! Careful! Where've you been? I thought you were upstairs working."

He pushes roughly past her, hears her greet Leah. "Didn't realize you two know each other!"

He runs up the stairs two at a time. Throws himself back on the bed. Turns off the light. His heart's still pounding.

His head feels like it will burst.

Don't think. Hold your breath. Count. Imagine you're in a cave. The tide's rising. Only way out is by swimming underwater into the next cave. There's a narrow tunnel through rock. No air. Count. Getting better. Over a minute now.

His pulse begins to slow down. Better. Back in control now. Just count.

4

Monday morning; the bus is late. Simon's missed registration. He signs the late list at the school office, and shoves and pushes his way through the seething corridors along with the other thousand people till he gets to class.

Some days he has to steel himself just to survive at school. It's like shutting down all the hatches one by one, battening down until you're just a hard shell. Nothing soft or vulnerable can be left showing or it will be mercilessly hunted down and slaughtered by someone. Kid or grown up. There's not much difference, it seems. The science teacher is one of the worst. And this is a decent school by most standards.

It's different for the girls, you can see. They talk to each other, and go around arm in arm, and make this ridiculous fuss if they're apart for a class, way over the top. It's not that he wants to do anything like that, of course, but he would at least like to feel *safe*. Still, he's got the rabbit to tell Johnny and Pike and Dan about today.

He joins the end of the ninth-grade crush outside the double doors of the two art rooms. He can't see Johnny or anyone, so he hangs back. Adam Skinner is sticking chewing gum into the back of Rachel Lintell's long hair. The seventh graders at the front of their line are squashed against the doors. Adam Skinner has turned his attention to a small group of seventh-grade boys who are playing catch with some girl's pencil case. There's always someone like Adam Skinner in your study group, whichever school you go to. Sometimes a lot more than one.

"In a *line*! No *pushing*!" Miss Jarvis arrives and takes her class in. You can still hear her shouting when the door's shut. She's leaving at the end of the term. Having a baby.

The ninth-grade line straightens itself and quiets down for no apparent reason. Mr. Davies strides down the corridor, and they file into their places in the art room. Almost everyone likes Mr. Davies. He doesn't shout. Doesn't need to. How? It's invisible, what he does, but he does something.

Johnny's saved Simon a place at the tables near the window. Simon slips into the chair, dumps his bag under the table. He keeps his coat on.

"I got a rabbit at the weekend," Simon tells Johnny.

"You never! What with?"

"Slingshot. Perfect aim. Middle of the head."

It sounds better that way. He doesn't go into the neckbreaking business.

"What did you do with it?"

"Skinned it, cooked it, ate it." Simon grins, triumphant.

Dan's leaning forward now. "What did you do with the skin?"

"Kept it. I'll show you later."

Mr. Davies is giving them that look. They shut up while he explains their task. They've been doing Surrealism this

38

term. Salvador Dali. Simon's favorite is the painting of a horse skeleton. It's called *The Happy Horse*. They've each worked on four different surreal designs, one of which will be painted full-scale. That's what they're doing today. It's a double lesson.

Mr. Davies holds up some of the designs to show the rest of the class. He doesn't mention names; that's another good thing about him. He doesn't pick on people, doesn't humiliate. Isn't sarcastic.

He holds up Simon's design of a fish finger on top of an iceberg for the class to discuss. Simon's good at drawing; an appreciative murmur goes round the art room, and Johnny digs him in the ribs.

Once everyone's busy with sketching out their pictures it's easy to drift off. Simon goes back to the field, the dead rabbit, then the cliff and his secret swim off the rocks. He's in the sort of dream-state the surrealists talk about; he lets his hand doodle over the paper in front of him, finds himself drawing the images in his mind. Gets quite carried away.

"I thought we'd decided on the iceberg?" Mr. Davies's voice pierces the shell he's surrounded himself with for the last half hour. "But never mind. This is good. Very good. Fine draftsmanship."

The rabbit looks real: each hair, the lie of the ears, its terrified eyes. Mr. Davies looks at Simon as if to take him in more closely. "The child and the savage . . ." he mutters under his breath. He moves on to the next table.

"What's he going on about?" Johnny asks Simon.

Simon shrugs. "No idea," he says, although in fact he does. It's what Dali thought painters should do: suspend the rational part of the mind, let the unconscious inform the painting. The primitive part of you. But it doesn't do to let on too much. It's OK to be good at art, as long as you're crap at other things, like math or English. Since he can't spell, he's OK. And now he can kill rabbits and stuff, too.

"It looks real. More real than real," Pike says. "You could sell that."

"It's sick, your drawing," Rachel Lintell says as she goes past their table on her way to the sink. "Cruel."

"You've got gum in your hair," Johnny says innocently, to irritate her. "Did you know?"

She flushes, bites her lip, pulls her long plait around to see the disgusting pink mess clogging the strands. It won't come out. They laugh. Simon thinks of the knife deep in his bag. You're not supposed to bring knives to school, but he never goes anywhere without his. He lets himself imagine cutting through the thick pleat of hair. The knife blade is sharpened on a steel. It could cut through hair easy as butter. *That slit up the rabbit's belly, the thin red line and the way the flesh opened out.*

"OK, everyone. Time to clean up before the bell. Don't forget to write down the homework for next class, please."

There's a sound like stampeding rhinos from the adjoining art room as the bell rings for the end of the class. Through the open door, Simon can see the seventh-grade teacher in the corridor, looking as if she's about to cry. Simon notices the way Mr. Davies goes and stands next to her; he puts his hand on her arm.

"Simon? Got a moment at the end of school today?" Mr. Davies asks as he's shuffling out of the art room. "For a very quick word. Nothing to worry about."

Simon shrugs. "OK." He runs to catch up the others

who are already disappearing down the corridor.

"Oi! No running!" a voice shouts above the din. He takes no notice.

"What does Davies want?" Johnny asks him.

"Don't know. I've got to see him after school."

"Nice!" Pike teases. "I bet he wants you to go into business with him. Make a fortune."

"Yeah, right!"

"He makes a mint, you know. As an artist. Got his own studio and everything. He's probably going to invite you there."

Dan joins in the laugh, and Simon hangs back, suddenly uncomfortable. He loathes the way you never really know how you stand, not even with your mates. Not when you're in school. Never know where the next insult's coming from. He can't seem to get tough enough not to mind.

In tutor group that afternoon the topic is "Safety Issues during Vacation." They have to watch a video produced by the government or someone, which has these stupid teenagers acting out an adult version of how young people behave, and it's so obviously phony. The teenagers are riding bikes by a canal, and one falls in and another nearly drowns because he wades in to save the first one even though he can't swim. The girls just panic on the bank, doing nothing and squealing a lot. It's supposed to teach them that you shouldn't try and save your mates when they fall in water. But what kind of mate would you be to stand on the side and say you were going to find a large log—maybe—that they could hang on to? Or, that you were running off to phone the fire department, so please hang on and don't drown in the meantime?

"Be serious!" Mrs. Fielding keeps saying. She tries to get them to discuss the issues, which starts everyone off on telling their worst-ever accident stories. They all love that. Adam Skinner tells a wonderful story about his brother playing on the railway line which may well be true, knowing Adam Skinner's brother, but Mrs. Fielding thinks he's making it up. Then Skinner tells the bit about where his brother's friend falls off a railway bridge and gets decapitated by an intercity train, and the class goes quiet and a bit twitchy, and the stories change to people they know who've died. Simon keeps quiet.

"I don't know why you're all so interested in death," Mrs. Fielding says at the end of tutor time. "Too many horror movies, no doubt."

Luke Butler makes his usual profound comments, like, "Well, it's what life's all about isn't it, Miss, death?"

She doesn't reply, but sums up her main lesson points: "So, don't hang out near water, railway lines, roads, building sites, cliffs, old quarries, or mineshafts. Not that many of you will ever move beyond the computer screen in your bedroom. So you'll be perfectly safe." She smiles to soften the dig. She has a personal vendetta against screens.

At the end of the day, Simon trails back along to the art department.

Mr. Davies is stacking cartridge paper away in the cupboard. He looks up and smiles.

"Thanks for coming. Won't keep you long. Got a bus to catch?"

Simon nods.

"Just wanted to say you did a fantastic piece of work this morning. I mean it. Truly outstanding. You've got real talent."

Simon looks at his feet. His ears are burning. "Thanks," he grunts.

"You've chosen art next year? For college placement?"

Simon nods.

"Good. You could really go somewhere with that sort of talent. Where d'you get that from, eh? Dad or Mum an artist?"

Simon shakes his head. "Mum's a learning support thingy."

"And Dad?"

Si clears his throat. The silence stretches out.

"No."

"There's something dark, something quite—" Mr. Davies fumbles for the right word "—*disturbing* in your work, isn't there? Quite a theme of yours, yes? The dead rabbit, and that skull you drew the other week, and the bird skeleton?"

Simon doesn't answer.

"What's that all about, then?"

Simon shrugs. "Nothing. It's just things I find, mostly."

Mr. Davies shrugs back. "You don't want to talk about it. That's fine. Why use words when you've got images, anyway?" He smiles. "Go on, then. Get your bus. But I'm usually here, end of the day, if you want to talk about anything."

Simon hurries out and up the drive to the bus stop. No one there; he's missed the bus, and all for nothing. The road is dusty. Each time a car passes, it stirs the small heaps of dry leaves which have fallen from the two horse chestnut trees at the end of the school drive. Conkers are already beginning to form: small green balls suspended from the twigs where the flowers were, back in May. The blacktop smells hot; everything has slowed down. The school looks strange with no kids, no noise.

What did he mean, "quite a theme of yours"?

No sign of a bus. Perhaps there isn't another one. It's not that far to walk. Better than waiting here. He shifts his backpack onto his shoulder and follows the route the bus would have taken, up to the main road, and then the lengthy trek along it. There's no pavement for the first stretch. Two delivery trucks thunder past, blasting their horns but not slowing down. Then there's a lull in traffic, and as he starts the downward stretch, the landscape opens out on one side; he can see over fields crisscrossed with drystone walls and stumpy windblown hedges all the way to the sea. Two buzzards wheel in a great arc over the moorland, calling their thin lonely *mew mew.*

There must be a quicker way back, rather than along this bleak strip of main road which follows the contours of the land, the more shallow gradient. *Need a map,* Simon thinks. There must be farm tracks, shorter, steeper ways over the land. Every so often he passes a gate, the faint mark of a track over grass, not signposted as a footpath, and maybe only the place where foxes or badgers have their runs. Or sheep. The moorland is dotted with them. Nothing much will grow here but grass and sedges, heather and gorse.

The land is pockmarked with outcrops of granite, the bones of the land jutting through its thin skin of turf.

There are the remains of old mines and quarry workings. Lines of mineshafts run underground, rotten and collapsed; it's a long time since any were used. Simon likes to imagine it when it was all heaving with life: men with stone-dusted faces climbing up out of the earth, horses pulling carts of stone; the chimneys smoking the air. The crank and crash of pulleys hauling trucks along a mineshaft.

Now there's no sign of human life except the occasional farm building. Far toward the horizon there's a square grey house with washing blowing in its windswept garden, and westward, a church tower nestling in a dip in the land, ringed by trees. From here they look like dark giants with their arms all stretched out one way. The wind has blown them into this shape.

Mr. Davies' house and studio are over there on the edge of the moor.

A farm truck roars past Simon, blasting its horn and spraying him with muck from the side of the road. He squeezes himself back against the hedge, swearing, his words caught in the rush of air the truck sucks in. He watches the truck slam on its brakes as it hits the bend in the road and skids slightly on the hot blacktop.

Just beyond the bend he can make out a small dirt track off to the left, between high hedge-topped walls. Anything has to be better than walking along this main road. It's impossible to get completely lost; there's always the line of the coast to follow, even if it does go the long way around, in and out and up and down every dip of the cliff. And there must be a quicker way straight across the fields.

Sweat trickles down his neck. He's still wearing his school sweater. He feels too exposed at school to take it off.

Nobody here, though. He shoves it in his bag. The sun beats down on his arms and neck; it's still high in the sky and there's hardly any shade. His shoes are grey with dust. The track runs at a right angle to the main road, straight toward the sea, going nowhere. No sign of houses or even farm buildings. He keeps going for a few hundred yards; there's a break in the stone wall, a stone stile, ancient and lichen-covered. A path, then. Yes—just a few yards further down there's another stile, the other side of the track. He's hit some old field path, and the right-hand branch is going roughly in the right direction. He'll risk it.

The first bit is easy enough: diagonally across the rough grass field there's another stone stile, into another small field. This one has sheep grazing in it; they look up at him with their narrow slitty eyes. He narrows his own, pretends to fire an imaginary crossbow, makes the hissing sound. The sheep wheel off, one after another, in alarm. Simon laughs out loud. They're so stupid, sheep.

The next stile isn't so obvious. He goes up and down the prickly hedge, searching for a way through. It takes a while. He finally pushes through a small gap, stinging himself on nettles as he clambers over a rusty line of barbed wire. This can't be the way. He glances at his watch: it's quarter to five already. He's normally home by now. He's too hot and thirsty, nothing left in his water bottle. He needs a spring, or even an animal trough. There's a way of getting to the clean water in a trough where it isn't contaminated by bugs and bacteria.

Aboriginal children are taught to memorize the water holes in their tribal territory. Cherokee Indians listen to the sound of water because they think it has a voice, telling them things.

This field is bone dry. His throat feels scratched by dust from the road. No wild strawberries here. The blackberries won't be ripe for weeks. He tries sucking a small hawthorn berry but it's dry and rough inside, no moisture. Simon sits down at the edge of the field. It's so still, so unbelievably silent. No birdsong, even, no traffic. Not even an airplane droning overhead, or the coastguard helicopter. He could be miles from anywhere. In the silence, he hears the faint rustling of leaves along the dry ditch: some small animal, a mouse or a shrew. He wishes he had the slingshot. There's bound to be rabbits.

He needs to find the path; this wasn't the right way through. He retraces his steps back through the hedge and the nettle patch.

Crack!

A single shot splits the silence. The echo ricochets along a stretch of stone wall at one edge of the field. Simon stops, shocked, heart thumping. He'd thought he was completely alone. Someone has been here all the time, watching him. Someone with a gun. Trying to frighten him? He turns slowly round. Still no one. It's hard to pinpoint exactly where the shot came from, the way it bounced and echoed off the granite. He stands, waits, listens.

A slight sound rustles behind him; he whips round. A shadow. The figure of a man.

It's as if he's appeared out of thin air. He has crept up without Simon hearing a thing, not until the very last minute. Simon's heart thuds. He wishes he had his knife in his hand.

The man's not that old, although his face is tanned and creased from being out in sun and wind and all weather.

He's got a shotgun under his arm, muzzle down. Old army boots. A torn shirt, grubby hands. His eyes are pale, watery, unfocused.

"What are you doing here?" His voice sounds rusty, as if he's not used to talking, and the hand holding the shotgun is shaking. The man keeps glancing round nervously.

Simon's mouth has gone dry. He can sense immediately that there's something strange about this man, something not right. He glances at the gun again. "I'm looking for the path—the stile. I thought there was a path across the fields." His voice comes out squeaky, all wrong.

The man's eyes focus briefly on Simon. "You shouldn't be here. It isn't safe. You keep away."

Fear prickles along Simon's neck. "Sorry," he stutters. "I just lost the path. . . ."

The man looks troubled by something Simon can't see. He's staring across the field, muttering. Simon looks in the same direction, but there's nothing there. The man's breathing heavily, his hand on the gun.

Close up, the man smells odd too. Not exactly disgusting, but a smell of earth, or metal, or something like that. Simon shifts away slightly. *Over there*, he thinks. *That looks like a way through the hedge. Just get away, fast. Make a run for it. Or maybe better to walk away quietly, steadily, so as not to be threatening or challenging, or whatever.* Something he saw on television flashes into his mind—an SAS guy coming across this remote tribe who were all armed with poisonous arrows; he had to keep very still and move slowly, show he wasn't a threat. They were that close to killing him. . . .

It's the worst feeling, turning your back when someone's got a gun. But there isn't any other option. The small field seems to have grown huge.

Nearly there.

The hedge has overgrown the stile completely, he can see as he gets close up. It's another stone one, with a broad slab across the top. Simon fumbles in his bag for his knife, to cut through the tough stalks of brambles and nettles. He can sense the man still watching him; it makes him clumsy. The knife feels good in his hand, though; the blade is sharp. He climbs through the hole he's cut, a tunnel through the hedge, and clambers over the granite stile. There's the faintest indentation in the grass on the other side to indicate where a path might be. He starts to run across the field.

A gate at the far end takes him onto a deeply rutted farm track which runs downhill toward a cluster of low grey buildings. It's the farm with the washing he saw from the road. He walks toward it, heart still thumping. A dog starts to bark. The track leads straight into a farmyard where chickens scratch and run freely; there's a car parked, a grey Citroën with rusting hubcaps. A woman comes and stands in the doorway of the farmhouse to see what's making the dog bark.

"You looking for someone?" She doesn't smile.

"No," Simon stammers. "I'm trying to find the path home. To town."

"Coast path's straight ahead, down the track. Or there's the Coffin Path, across the fields. I wouldn't go that way, not by myself." She folds her arms over her apron, like somebody in an old horror film. Black and white.

Simon doesn't hang around. He takes the track to the coast path. So what if it's longer?

At last he can see the houses at the edge of the town, the beginning of the paved path, and proper benches, and trashcans, and the rough track he can take to short-cut back up to the edge of the town where their house is. He's desperate for a drink.

He glances at the girl's house; she's not there tonight. The door's shut. But his is wide open, and Nina is standing there. She doesn't smile or wave or anything as he comes up the hill.

"Sorry I'm late." Pre-emptive strike.

"Where the hell have you been? You're *hours* late. I phoned Johnny and then Dan, and even Pike, and they finally remembered something about the art teacher and then I phoned school and he wasn't there and I ended up having to phone him at his home address and he said you'd left school well before four. You don't *think*, do you? And look at the state of you! That white top! You'll have to wash that before tomorrow, you haven't got another one and you can't go in looking like that—"

"I said I'm sorry."

"Don't use that tone with me! I was on the verge of getting the police out for you!"

"Just *slightly* over the top. I missed the bus, so I walked. Big deal. And I tried to do a short cut but it ended up longer. Made a mistake. Sorry. And now I'm desperate for a drink—OK?"

He pushes past her into the kitchen, drops the bag en route, shoves his head under the running tap to gulp in cold water. It trickles down his chin; he closes his eyes. He can't tell her about that strange man now. She's already too worked up.

Nina stumbles over the dumped bag in the dark corridor; the knife slips out onto the floor. She picks it up.

"What's *this* doing in your school bag? You know you're forbidden to carry knives at school. What's gotten into you, Simon? This is ridiculous!"

She slumps in a kitchen chair. She looks as if she's about to cry. Or get really angry. He sits down opposite her, in the place that is still set for supper. Nina and Ellie have already eaten. He closes his eyes while she goes on and on and on.

The phone rings. Nina answers it, Simon half listens from upstairs. She's talking about him. She laughs, a new, different note in her voice. He stops listening. Lies back on the bed, head resting on his hands.

It's still light, though the sun's almost set. Perfect for going out with the slingshot. An air rifle would be even better. The field will be covered in rabbits, young ones who don't know much about danger yet. Don't run when they first see him crouched in the shadow of the hedge. He thinks again of the weird man, that single shot echoing out across the fields. Who is he?

Nina stands in the doorway of his room. "We must get those curtains fixed up," she says.

He doesn't say anything.

"Finished your homework?"

He nods, although he hasn't done any.

"That was your art teacher. Kind of him, don't you think? Phoning to check you were safely back. Beyond the call of duty, I reckon. He said some nice things about you. Your work. Well done, Si." She smiles.

Is she about to hug him? He hopes not.

51

"Matthew Davies. 'Call me Matt,' he said. He's got a lovely voice. What was he talking to you about after school, anyway?"

"Art."

"Well, yes. But what exactly?"

"I don't know. Just stuff. He asked if you were an artist."

"Me? What did you say?"

"No, of course."

"Oh." She sounds disappointed. What is the matter with her these days?

"He's invited me in for a chat too."

"Why?"

"Because you're *very talented*, he says. We should discuss your future. That's really good, Si. That he's taking special notice of you."

"Don't go on about it. OK? Don't make such a big deal of everything."

He watches the window darken. Stars come out. The Big Dipper, and the North Star, and the three stars of Orion's Belt.

Just before he falls asleep he sees again the figure of the man, hears the shot ring out. The man was trying to scare him off, wasn't he? He wasn't shooting rabbits or foxes. Simon thinks about Johnny's dad's gun, and the instruction manual they'd pored over, him and Pike and Johnny after school one afternoon. The warning, printed in black, bold letters: *Danger of Death.*

It's everywhere. There's nowhere safe. Better to be prepared. Ready. Better to be armed.

5

Simon wakes up late, in a foul mood. He's had that dream again, the one where he's underground, in some sort of tunnel, and the roof collapses, and he's trapped in the suffocating dark. But this time he's not alone. Someone else is trapped with him, and coming closer. He's sweating all over, his heart racing.

He's always had dreams, ever since he was really little, even before his father died. They got worse after that. He'd wake up screaming in the night. Except that he wasn't properly awake, even though his eyes were wide open; he couldn't hear or see anything. Not even his mother. "It was as if you were somewhere else, somewhere I couldn't reach you, to call you back," she said.

This morning it feels as if he's doing everything in slow motion: getting washed and dressed, and packing his bag for school. He still hasn't done any homework. It's so near the end of school now he can't be bothered. He slips his knife into the bottom of the bag. It makes him feel safer, just knowing it's there. Today he's going to take in the rabbit skin to show Dan and Johnny and Pike. It's wrapped in some newspaper on his bedroom table. When he picks it up he realizes it's starting to smell funny. He must've done something wrong. It shouldn't smell at all.

"Hurry up!" Nina keeps shouting up the stairs. " You're going to be late."

"Don't forget, will you?" she says as she leaves for work. "You're collecting Ellie from Rita's, so I can go straight from work to that meeting with your teacher. Yes?"

He grunts.

He hates going to Rita's. Rita is Ellie's babysitter. She's lived in the town ever since she was a child and she knows everyone. She's kind and Ellie loves her. Nina calls her a godsend. Nina pretends not to like gossip, but Simon reckons she enjoys hearing Rita talking about everyone the way she does.

Simon hates the way she asks you questions. And the way she knows things without you even telling her.

The trapped, suffocating feeling from the dream stays with him all day. He can't concentrate properly in class. No one seems to notice. At lunchtime they lie out on the grass and he shows people the rabbit skin. It looks pathetic, the thin strip of dried skin and fur, and the smell makes everyone retch. He tosses it in the trash. The little kids are playing a game called "Deathball."

"Everyone want to come back to our place after school?" Pike asks.

They do. Just in time, Simon remembers about Ellie.

"All right, Simon?" Rita asks as she answers the door. "Haven't seen you for a while. How's school?"

"OK."

"Not long till vacation, eh?"

Ellie winds herself around Rita's legs, thumb in her mouth. Rita unwinds her, gives her a quick hug. "She's been telling me about your neighbor. Leah Sweet. She's going to be the new babysitter, I understand." Rita laughs, as if there's some sort of private joke.

"Still, that's nice for Leah. She could do with the money, I bet. And a bit of company. What with her mother and everything, you know? So, what's Leah doing these days? She's left school now, I suppose? They leave as soon as they've done their placement exams these days, don't they? She going to college, then?"

He shrugs. How's he supposed to know?

"What time's Nina back? I'll give her a call later."

He squirms. "Dunno," he says.

"Well, what's she doing? A meeting, she said. Work?"

"At my school," Simon mumbles. "With a teacher."

"Oh dear! Hope you're not in trouble!" Rita chuckles.

Ellie chirps up. "No. It's because he's good at art—"

"Shut up, Ellie," he growls.

Ellie's lip quivers. *Get away, quick,* he thinks, *before she starts crying.* "Come on, Ellie. Piggyback?"

He can be nice when he tries. She is only little, after all. He can remember what it's like, just. He crouches down so she can climb onto his back and then he straightens up quickly on purpose to make her squeal and hang on really tight.

"You're strangling me, Ellie! Hold my shoulders, not my neck!"

He lets her play horsie all the way home. He's the horse, and she has to tell him which way to go and say things like "Giddy-up!" and "Whoa there!" It's one of the games he can remember playing with his dad.

The girl—Leah—is leaning over her gate. Ellie scrabbles to get down off his back and runs over to her. Simon dawdles, watching them. They've obviously been getting to know each other. It's so easy for Ellie, talking to people. She doesn't care what they think. But it looks as if Leah likes Ellie; she's smiling at her as she chatters on. Once or twice she glances towards Simon. He pretends to be looking for his front-door key in his bag.

What was Rita going on about just now? It's not really surprising that she knows Leah. It's a small enough town when the tourists aren't around. But what did she mean about her mother?

He hasn't ever seen Leah's mother. Not that he can remember. Not that he's been looking, or anything. But it's odd, when they live just across the road. He knows most of the people in this bit of the road by sight, at least. And he's seen a man who must be Leah's father, leaving early in the morning sometimes. He drives a white van.

"Hi, Simon." Leah's voice teases him. He has to speak now. He can feel the blood race up his neck and into his face. He must look totally stupid.

"Hi." His voice comes out OK this time. He dives through the gate and into the house.

Ellie bounces in after him a few minutes later. "Look what Leah gave me!" She holds out a hairclip in the shape of a butterfly. Pretty. Before he can stop himself, he's imagining it in Leah's hair, the feel of undoing it so the hair sweeps back over her face. He blushes, snaps at Ellie. "You shouldn't take presents from strangers."

"She's not a stranger, silly. She's Leah. She's my friend."

"No she's not."

"She is. And she's going to babysit for me."

"That doesn't make her a friend."

Ellie gives up. "What's for tea?"

"I don't know, do I? Get yourself something to eat."

"When's Mummy back?" Her lip quivers slightly. "I want Mummy."

Simon pours himself a bowl of cereal and takes it into the sitting room in front of the TV. Ellie tags on behind. She's filled her bowl too full; milk sloshes over the edge onto the carpet. They watch the end of *Neighbours*, flip to *The Weakest Link* and then *The Simpsons*. Ellie's sniveling. He doesn't look at her.

A car pulls up outside. Ellie goes to the window; she runs out to fling herself at Nina.

"Sorry, sweetheart. Didn't mean to be this late. How was your day?"

Simon shoves the door so it slams shut, cutting off their voices, but Nina opens it again almost immediately.

"Hello, Si. OK?"

He grunts.

"Thanks for getting Ellie."

Grunts again.

"Don't you want to know what Mr. Davies said?"

"I'm watching this."

"All right. Get the message. Later. I'll start supper."

"What is it?"

"Don't know yet." She closes the door.

Ellie's hopping up and down the hallway, making a racket. He turns up the volume. It's a repeat, of course. He's seen them all by now. When it's over he slouches along to the kitchen. Ellie's already at the table, drawing figures with big heads and things that might be ears, or possibly wings.

"What's for supper?"

"Sausages, chips, and peas. All out of the freezer. You could've been doing it while you were waiting for me to get back, then it wouldn't have been so late. Set the table, will you?"

"Why me? How come you never ask her to do anything?"

"Because she's six and you're fourteen. You didn't have to do it when you were six."

Nina's voice is clipped. He knows what she's not saying. *When he was six, everything was different. His father was still there. She, Nina, wouldn't be doing absolutely everything single-handedly. And Ellie wasn't even born.*

"Can't we eat in front of the TV?"

Nina frowns. "But I wanted us to talk. About your drawings. Matt Davies . . . Oh, all right, then. Get on with you. Take everything in on a tray." She spoons peas onto the waiting plates.

Simon grabs the tomato ketchup from the fridge and takes his plate into the front room. Ellie follows. She thrusts her picture at Simon. "It's for you. A present."

"What's it supposed to be?"

"It's a picture of Leah, silly."

He crumples it in one hand. Ellie starts to snivel. Nina sits down next to her on the sofa, puts one arm round her. "Don't take any notice, bunnikins. He's a crosspatch today."

Simon flicks the channels, finds some program called

The Tudor War Machine. It shows you how to make salt-peter for gunpowder out of horse dung, black earth, and piss. Some guy in a foundry casts a Tudor-style cannon and they test-fire it on Salisbury Plain. It has to be done by remote control in case the whole thing blows up.

Nina keeps interrupting to tell Simon things about the art teacher. "You're lucky being taught by a real artist," she says. "He's passionate about art, isn't he?"

The replica Tudor cannonball has shot through the wooden target, leaving a jagged hole. In oak, like on a Tudor battleship, the guy says, those splinters would be deadly.

"—so he invited me to have a look round."

"What?"

"His studio. You haven't been listening to anything I've been saying, have you?" Nina slides Ellie off her lap. "Come on, sleepyhead. Let's get you to bed." She turns back from the doorway. "Oh yes, and he says you're late with some homework. So turn that off and get on with it."

He scowls.

The phone rings. And rings. Simon ignores it; it won't be for him, anyway. He hates talking on the phone.

Nina's feet clatter down the wooden stairs. She glares at Simon through the half-open door. "You could have—" But she's picked it up now. "Rita!" she says instead. "How are you?"

Simon half listens to Nina's side of the conversation.

"Why? What did she say?"

"Oh!"

"And the mother?"

"No wonder. Poor Leah."

"Yes, I understand. Thanks, Rita. See you then, bye."

She stands for a moment in the dark hallway next to the silent phone. Simon watches her, but he says nothing. What does she mean, *poor Leah*?

Then he wonders why he's even bothering to think about it. It's bugging him, the way Leah's getting everywhere. He tugs his art book out of his school bag and flips through the pages already filled with drawings. Pencil, mostly. He knows they're good. The sheep's skull, and the dead bird, and part of an ammonite. There's a detailed drawing of his Black Widow slingshot. He doodles around on one of the blank pages, a sort of arrowhead shape. The he draws a head and shades in the long hair, so that starts turning into Leah too. He scribbles over it, messing it up. That means he has to rip it out of the book. What was the homework? A still life. That's what he always draws, isn't it? Things that aren't alive. Still lives.

His school bag still stinks of rotting rabbit skin. He sniffs his fingers. They smell too. He goes out to the kitchen and washes his hands over and over under cold water. He doesn't bother to turn the light on.

He can hear muffled sobs coming from Ellie's room. He tramps upstairs and stands in Ellie's doorway. Her light's still on; she has it on till after she's asleep, and then the door must be left open so the landing light can shine in.

"Still awake?"

More sobs.

"Sorry about your drawing," he says. "Will you do me another one tomorrow?"

Ellie pokes her face out from under the covers. She

nods.

"Night night, then."

Nina's door is shut. She's still pissed off with him about something. He can't remember what.

Across the road, Leah watches the pattern of lights in the Piper household. By ten thirty, all the downstairs ones are off. There are two still on upstairs, and one stays on till at least midnight, when she, Leah, eventually falls asleep. She sleeps lightly, wakes when an owl hoots across the dark garden, still half dreaming. Something about a butterfly, and a feeling of being tangled up, caught so she can't break free. It's hot in her bedroom; she pads across to the window to open it wide, and sees that the light in Mrs. P's room is still on. The clock says one fifteen.

She lies back down on the bed, kicks the covers off. Where she left a gap in the curtains, the silvery light of a nearly full moon shines in on her naked body, sculpts her limbs in silver shadows. She has that feeling again, of something pressing in, coming closer. The owl hoots again. She's like someone in a film, she thinks. The heroine, whose life is about to be changed completely as she is woken to love, to life. She smiles, turns over, sleeps again.

6

Simon scans the pages of the old newspaper lying on the kitchen table while he spreads golden syrup on his toast.

City in fear. Drunken youths rampage through town center. . . .

Schoolboy, 16, found hanging in bedroom. . . .

Policeman arrested on Internet child pornography charges. . . .

"Bring back our boys!" say military wives. . . .

Nina is washing up the breakfast things, singing along to the radio, sounding horribly cheerful.

"Si? I'm going out tonight. Can you make sure to be in, to look after Ellie?"

"What! Mum! It's Friday!"

"Well, yes, I know. And for once, I'm going out. Or I'd like to. Seeing as it's my first invitation out, almost, since we've been in this house."

"Where?" Simon's suspicious.

"Matt asked me for supper."

"*Matt?*" He can hardly believe his ears.

"Matt Davies. Art teacher. Yes."

"What on earth for?"

Nina smiles. "I guess he took pity on me, poor single mother with a son like you, Simon, newly moved into the town. He seems a compassionate sort of guy." She laughs, but Simon is not joining in. This is serious.

"You can't go out with a *teacher*, Mum. Not one from my school."

"It's not going out with him, silly. It's just supper, with other people. OK? Do I have your permission?" She laughs again, flicks her hair back from her face.

Simon scowls back. "But it's Friday. I always go out with Dan and Johnny and Pike. It's not fair. Why should I have to look after Ellie?"

Nina sighs. "I'll get a babysitter, then. OK?"

He doesn't bother to answer. He picks up his bag for school, takes a banana from the bowl on the cupboard, slams the door. He thinks about Nina as he makes his way to the bus stop. *Might've guessed she'd do something like this. Majorly embarrassing. Supposing someone at school finds out? I'll have to keep well away from the art rooms.*

That's not difficult, as it turns out. It's so near the end of school now they're hardly doing any work. He volunteers to help the PE teacher clear out Lost Property instead of going to math and then art. Math will just be a video anyway. He'd have been finishing his painting in art, and he feels a stab of disappointment and then anger at Nina. The painting's good. He knows that. Now he won't have time to finish it. Her bloody fault. Simon broods over it as he sifts through mud-stained PE shirts and stinking sneakers and gym shorts, sorting them into piles: named, unnamed, good condition, rubbish.

The day gets worse.

Afternoon registration. He waits until Mrs. Fielding has finished calling the names and handing out notices, then leans across the scratched, graffiti-covered tabletop to talk to Johnny, a row in front.

"Should we plan our camping trip, then?" he asks him.

Pike and Dan turn round to listen.

"What's this, then?"

Something in Pike's tone makes Simon uncomfortable. "Camping. First week of vacation. Like we said, remember?"

"Well, it wasn't definite or anything. It seemed a good idea at the time. But it's different now," Johnny says.

"What do you mean?"

"Well, now my mum and dad have planned vacation and everything. We're going the first week, soon as school breaks up. Northern Spain."

"Well, the week after, or the next one after that, it doesn't really matter when," Simon says, even though it does.

Pike chips in. "We're going to be sailing."

"We're going straight off too," Dan says. "France. So I can't go camping either."

They don't want to go with me. Why would they when they can do all these really exciting things abroad, with proper families? They've changed their minds and not told me, and now I look a complete idiot.

If he weren't at school he'd feel like crying. He wouldn't, of course. He hasn't cried for a really long time. So long, he can't even remember the last time. *They don't want to be friends any more. They're moving on without me.*

Well they can get lost. What kind of friends are they anyway?

The bell rings for the first class after lunch. Just as he's packing his stuff back into his bag Mrs. Fielding calls him up to her desk.

"Why weren't you in your art lesson this morning?" she says.

He explains about helping the PE teacher.

She frowns. "Not a very good reason, Simon. You shouldn't be missing classes. Anyway, Mr. Davies wants to see your homework. You'd better take it to the art room at the end of the day."

He doesn't tell her he hasn't done it.

Johnny, Dan, and Pike have already gone ahead in the general rush out of the classroom. Simon lets himself be washed along with a tide of school kids down the corridor. It's scary, the way you get swept along by the mob whether you want to or not. *Imagine being in a fire with this bunch. You'd probably be trampled to death.* Just as an experiment, not really thinking, he pushes against the fire exit door as he's swept by. To his surprise the door swings open onto the parking lot at the side of the school, and he finds himself stumbling through. He stands there, dazed, and then starts walking across the blacktop. He keeps going, straight up the drive and out along the road. It's not premeditated. It simply seems the obvious thing to do. In the circumstances.

He glances back. No one has seen, no one's coming after him. He lopes off down to the second bus stop, not the one nearest the school gates, and he gets lucky: a bus pulls up after only about five minutes.

"Early closing, is it?" the driver raises an eyebrow at Simon.

"Dentist appointment."

"Ah. Sit down, then."

So what if the driver doesn't believe him? It's none of his business.

Simon hunches down in the back seat. The bus is almost empty. It rattles along, takes the corners too fast, judders as it climbs the hill and then squeals, braking, on the last long hill down into the town.

All the way he can't stop thinking.

Why didn't Pike and Dan and Johnny say anything about vacation before? What's going on?

They must have all been talking about me when I wasn't there. I'm still the new guy; they've all known each other for years. They've closed ranks.

But why? What've I done?

He tries a different tack. *Perhaps it isn't like that. Perhaps it's simply that they've got other plans, family things. It doesn't mean anything. They can't really help it. It happens all the time during vacation: real families doing things together.*

Sometimes, he feels as if he's completely alone. That Nina and Ellie don't count. That they're not a real family at all.

He gets off the bus at the church in the middle of town and slouches along the narrow street past the newsstand and the post office, cutting through the alley to the main street. It looks different this time of day, mostly old people shopping with those baskets on wheels that stab you in the back of the legs if you happen to get in the way. He's too conspicuous here; he takes off his school sweatshirt and stuffs it into his backpack, then takes the series of passages which cut through to the lower street and the path down to the beach. He skulks along, kicking Coke cans and pebbles, hands in pockets, shirt hanging loose. He can feel the smooth slim shape of his knife in the bag against his back. Feels good. A reminder of something about himself, something that gets lost when he's at school.

Seems like he's not the only one bunking off this afternoon. As he comes around the harbor wall he sees a knot of boys about his age crouched over something. Go back? Around? Too late. A familiar shape wheels around.

"Look who it isn't. Simple Simon."

Simon swears under his breath.

"You what? Come again?" Rick Singleton threatens.

He's wearing baggy shorts, T-shirt. Hasn't been to school, then. Or maybe the posh school's already broken up for the summer?

They're all crouched around a seagull, Simon can see now. A young one, still with its mottled brown plumage, its huge ugly beak squawking for food, too stupid to realize that these boys aren't going to help it. One of its wings trails broken and useless. Simon starts walking again. But he's yanked back suddenly as Rick catches the strap on his backpack.

"Where you going?"

"Just walking."

"Bit early, aren't you? Not cutting school, are we? What you got in that bag?"

"Nothing."

Rick yanks it again, as if to pull it off, but Simon anticipates it and holds on tight. Rick catches hold of one trailing sleeve of the school sweatshirt instead and pulls it out, runs off with it, laughing, rolls it into a tight ball and flings it out over the water. The green sweater unravels in its flight through the air, makes a flat splash in the shallow water, joins the other flotsam and jetsam bobbing between the mooring ropes at the edge of the harbor.

Simon could retrieve it easily, a sodden stinking bundle of cloth. But he doesn't. He runs. He keeps on running till he's quite sure there are no footsteps pounding after him. No sign of Rick. He must have rejoined the group clustered round the damaged seagull. Simon hates himself for running like that. But what else could he do?

That's twice he's seen him in less than a week. The thought that Rick Singleton and his new friends might be hanging around town all summer weighs in his guts like stone along with everything else. His heart's still hammering. He runs on until he's slipped past the end of the harbor wall and around onto the next bit of beach. The wind hits him. Salt, stinging.

A small crab scuttles sideways along the ridges of sand left by the retreating tide. Simon watches it for a minute. It doesn't have anywhere to go. He picks it up, his fingers positioned expertly round its shell so the pincers can't reach him, and carries it to the edge of the water. It flounders for a moment, then starts to bury itself in the wet sand.

He turns back, climbs up the sloping sea wall on to the road, cuts back home the long way up the hill.

"Si? Phone." Nina yells up the stairs.

"Who is it?"

"Johnny, I think. Hurry up. You been sleeping up there or what?" She passes him the phone. It's dusted white where her flour-covered hands have been holding it.

"Hello?"

"Simon? It's Johnny. Coming out later?"

"OK."

"Meet you usual place, yes? Bring your slingshot."

"OK."

"What happened this afternoon? Where did you go?"

"Tell you later. What time?"

"Seven thirty?"

"OK. See you."

Simon goes into the kitchen. Nina's spreading tomato purée on rolled-out pizza dough. She looks up. "So you are going out, then?"

"Yes."

"What time? So I can tell Leah when to come over."

"Leah? What?"

"She's babysitting tonight."

"Mum! Why did you have to ask her?"

"Well, who else am I supposed to ask? Anyway, Ellie's thrilled. And Leah's happy to earn a bit of extra money. Don't look like that. You did have the option, remember?"

"But, Mum! Her!"

"You don't have to have anything to do with her. You can be out before she arrives. And as soon as you get back, she can go. I'll pay her till ten. You're not to stay out any later than that. OK?"

"So I do have to see her, then, don't I?"

"For heaven's sake, Simon! Give us a break. Now I'm going to put these pizzas in the oven and then I'll get changed ready to go out. And don't you dare go all moody on me now. It'll spoil my whole evening."

Simon slumps in front of the TV. He flicks channels:

commercials, a nanosecond of some soap, *Robot Wars*.

"Get the pizza out, Si?" Nina calls down the stairs, "and serve it?"

He burns his hand on the oven tray, swears. Ellie watches him with round eyes. They both eat in silence at the kitchen table.

Ellie pushes her plate to one side. "Finished."

Simon reaches out and picks up her remaining slices, puts them on his own plate. Ellie watches.

"What are you staring at?" Simon asks her.

"You're not babysitting me. Leah is."

"Lucky Leah. Not. Anyway, you'll be in bed."

Ellie sticks her tongue out.

"Stop it, you two." Framed in the kitchen doorway, Nina looks like someone else. Her hair's different; she's got makeup on. She smiles.

"Mummy!" Ellie gets down from her chair and goes to hug her.

"Careful, Ellie. Your fingers are all tomatoey."

"You look lovely." Ellie strokes Nina's arm, twists the silver bangle round her wrist. "And you smell nice."

Simon turns away in disgust. He shoves his chair back so that it scrapes across the tiled floor, and pushes past them into the pantry.

He picks up his bag from the floor, pulls out the school books and leaves them in a messy heap, collects his slingshot from the high shelf.

"Have a good time, then, Si. And be careful. Where will you be? The field? Johnny's house?"

"Field."

"Back by ten at the absolute latest, Simon. Yes? Before

it gets dark."

"Yes. Yes. Yes."

It's way too early. Johnny won't be there for another half hour at least, so Simon walks slowly along the lane and across the path to the field. He can get some practice shots in before the others turn up. If they do.

The slingshot makes a thwacking sound. He fires small pebbles at the drystone wall at the end of the field. Some get embedded in the soft soil caught between the herring-bone layers of stones. He picks them out. Each of these stones has been chosen and laid by hand, the real hand of someone who lived and worked here. Dead now. This land is full of signs of the dead. There are ancient crosses and the burial mounds of Neolithic people. Standing stones. Ancient paths.

Footsteps. Simon swings around. Johnny's crossing the field, an air rifle bag slung over one shoulder.

"OK?"

"OK. Your dad let you borrow it?" He points at the air rifle.

"Yeah."

"Where are the others?"

"Busy. So, what happened? Did you blow off school?"

"Yes."

"Why?"

"Dunno. Just did. Just walked out."

"No one noticed."

"Great, thanks. So no one gives a shit."

"Stress-y! I meant teachers. We covered for you. We're friends, remember?"

"Oh."

"You're still mad with us about vacation."

Simon shrugs. "It doesn't matter—" He stops midsentence; ahead of them, two rabbits have hopped out of the hedgerow and are grazing the short grass at the edge of the field. Simon takes aim.

Johnny unzips the air rifle slip at just the wrong moment and the rabbits scarper. The stone goes wide.

"Sorry," Johnny says. "My fault."

"Loser!" Simon shoves him against the hedge, and Johnny swears.

"Bloody nettles."

Simon feels better. At least Johnny came out. He's OK, Johnny is.

"The other day," Simon says, "there was this guy. Not here, another field, farther along. With a gun. A really strange guy, a sort of tramp, but not old."

"Mad Ed," Johnny says, nodding. "Everyone knows him. He's weird as hell. You want to stay away from him. He's been in trouble with the police. He's a sad loner. Head case."

"What's wrong with him?"

"Something happened. Iraq or somewhere. The first Gulf War, in the nineties. His brother got killed. There's stories. His dad was a nut too, but that was to do with the Second World War. Shellshock or nerve gas or something. He's dead now too."

"He shouldn't be allowed a gun license," Simon says.

"He works on a farm, doesn't he?" Johnny replies, as if that explains everything.

They start collecting dead branches and armfuls of bracken to make a sort of camouflaged blind. They lean the branches against the trunk of an oak tree and weave the bracken in and out and then pile it on all over. It looks good. Crouched inside, they take potshots at a wizened hawthorn tree. There's a knot in the bark halfway up, perfect for target practice. Simon gets it six times out of seven with the slingshot. Johnny's not so good with the air rifle. But he gets better with practice. He lets Simon have a go.

It's beginning to get dark. The birds start flying home to roost. The sky over to the edge of the land pales to lilac. There's a distant *chug chug* of a fishing trawler coming around the bay into the harbor.

A magpie alights on a branch of their hawthorn tree.

"Mine," Johnny whispers.

The rifle shot echoes out over the darkening field and seems to hang in the cool air. A few feathers float down from the branch.

Simon blinks. *It's that easy, killing something.*

Johnny runs forward to find the still-warm body. Simon watches him searching through the patch of thistles and nettles at the foot of the tree. "Where did it fall?" he yells back to Simon. "Did you see? I definitely hit it."

From his distant position, Simon scans the tree. The dead bird is somehow plastered to the branch, a mass of black and white feathers stuck there.

"Weird, that," Johnny says when Simon points it out. "How come it just stays there?"

The killing seems less fun without the body.

Johnny pulls out a bottle of hard cider from his backpack. They drink it sitting in the lee of the drystone wall, and it's well after dark before they stagger back home across the fields bathed in silver moonlight.

7

Leah lies on her bed, carefully positioned so that the
moonlight shines directly onto the open diary she's been
writing for the last half hour. Her parents have long since
gone to bed, but she doesn't want to put the light on. The
silvery light through the open window is so much more ro-
mantic. The bedroom, with its plain walls and cheap furniture, is softened and smoothed by the deep shadows. She
reads back what she's written so far.

*Just got back from the Pipers' place. Read Ellie (sweet!)
loads of stories. Her room has shelves full of books! And this
really cute nightlight, with a moon and stars that glow. When
she was asleep (took ages) had a good look around. Went in
Simon's room. Weird, looking at this house from over there.
Nothing much to see in S's room. Boys' stuff like old models and
junk. Air-gun magazines. A horrible smelly old sheep skull and
lots of smaller ones. Birds or mice? And lots of drawings of dead
things. Mrs. P's was more interesting. Photo of a man by her
bed looks like Simon: maybe his dad? Lots of rings and bracelets
and earrings in the chest of drawers, but no letters. The room
looks tidy and a bit bare, but inside the drawers it is a real*

mess!!! Tried on some of her shoes but they were too small. Mrs. P says call her "Nina." Nina came back before Simon, who was supposed to be in by ten but wasn't. Where was he? I think she is too soft on him. A man drove Nina home, but I didn't see whether they kissed or not. She said she was over the limit but she didn't seem drunk to me. She gave me extra on account of being later than we said. I made almost twenty pounds and all for just having a nice time snooping around and reading a few stories!!!

While she was there she'd pretended it was her house, and she'd planned how she would decorate it. Simply, with just a few colors, like terracotta in the living room, and a sort of lilac-y lavender for the main bedroom. White sheets and white bedspread, and fine white gauzy curtains to blow in the breeze.

Leah sits up; she can hear a woman's voice shouting. She creeps to the open window to look out. In the house opposite, Simon's window is also open. Nina's raised voice echoes through the still night air. She's yelling something at Simon. He must have just gotten home. Nina sounds furious, although Leah can't hear the actual words. She glances at the clock. Twenty past eleven. Where has he been all this time?

He seems quite nice really. Pity he's so young. He's good looking in a shy sort of way. Tongue tied. He needs drawing out of himself.

Leah considers making him her summer project. She's so bored. It will fill in the time while she waits for the real man to come into her life. Yes, a project will be fun. *Look out, Simon Piper!!!*

Briefly, just before she goes to sleep, she wonders about the man who drove Nina home. She's seen him somewhere before, not just around the town like you do, but somewhere else. The TV? On a poster?

It's as if she has some special power, as if by thinking about him she has conjured him up. Leah's shopping for her mother, who's "ill" again. The town is crowded; it's Saturday morning. Local people doing ordinary shopping for food rub shoulders with vacationers looking for something to do on a damp morning. It starts to drizzle more heavily.

Leah wants to get out of the rain, but she hasn't enough money to spare for the café. And then, ahead of her in the street, she sees him. At least, she's almost certain it's him: a man with dark hair, short-sleeved linen shirt, blue shorts, leather boots. He pushes the door open into the bookshop on the main street, and Leah just follows.

She has never been in here before. There are two rooms, full of bookcases. Her shoes squeak on the wooden floorboards. There are comfortable chairs and a patterned rug in one corner, as if it's someone's sitting room. A bowl of sweetpea flowers stands next to the register. A carousel of postcards, art cards, to one side. Leah absorbs it all as if it's in a magazine.

The young woman behind the register looks up and smiles a greeting. "Hello, Matt."

She smiles at Leah too.

Matt. That's his name, then. It's definitely him, the man who brought Nina home last night. She follows him through the arch into the second room, to shelves labeled

"Art and Architecture."

This room is smaller. Standing so close (she's at "Fiction by Author A–H"), Leah can detect a faint delicious smell, not aftershave or soap, something more unusual, like earth. Clay, perhaps, or charcoal. Something arty.

Leah picks up a novel at random and pretends to read the blurb on the back.

His dark hair curls over his collar at the back. Not trendily short, but still attractive. His hands, holding a large hardback book with a shiny black cover, are tanned. Strong, capable hands, with thin fingers. Artist's hands, sensitive to the shape of things, used to carving out figures from stone or clay or wood. Leah feels a sudden tingle run right down her spine. Her heart pounds. She tips her head slightly, so that a curtain of hair sweeps down over one side of her face and covers up the spreading flush.

She moves farther away, takes the book over to one of the chairs near the window. Rain beats against the glass. Self-consciously she opens the book and reads the beginning. Words swim in front of her eyes, dance, blur. Nothing makes sense. She's aware of the man really close, flipping pages of the book in his hands. Every so often he seems to glance in her direction.

She gets up abruptly, pushes her book back into its space on the shelf, and rushes out of the shop onto the wet street. The woman at the register says something as she leaves, but she doesn't stop to listen.

Rain trickles down her neck, beads her eyelashes. The cool air feels delicious. She glances back through the bookshop window as she passes, and there he is, watching her.

She goes hot again. It's a new feeling, a mix of confusion, excitement and curiosity. *What does it mean?*

She forgets the shopping and makes her way instead down the high street and through the alley into the lower street and then down the stone steps on to the road that runs along next to the main beach.

Leah finds an empty bench in one of the shelters. A seagull lands right by her, squawks for food. Above the sea, the clouds are thinning. The rain will stop soon. Already there are more figures down on the beach. A dog races around and around after gulls, and two small children chase after the dog.

The seagull has perched itself on one arm of the bench. It watches her with its beady eye. Leah flaps her arms at it. "Shoo!"

It flaps back, moves off for a moment, and then returns. There are notices all along the seafront admonishing tourists, "Do NOT feed the seagulls." People tell stories about the things they do. "They'll take your sandwich right out of your hand." "A mob of seagulls pecked a baby and killed it." Leah watches the gull back. Its beak is huge when you see it close up. Hooked, vicious.

She could do with a drink. Something to eat. The kiosks along the shore sell ice creams, chips, greasy burgers that make your stomach turn. She could get something from the town, but she can't be bothered. What will Matt be doing now? Bought that flashy art book, perhaps, and then gone to a café for an espresso.

Simon scuffs along the town beach. His jeans are soaked; the legs act like a sort of wick, sucking up water from the puddles he makes no effort to avoid. He's seen her, the girl. Leah. In one of the shelters. He keeps his head down, but she's already spotted him. She's waving. She does that flick thing with her hair.

"Hi, Simon!"

He grunts. Keeps walking, head down.

She slides off the bench and picks her way over the wet sand toward him. Heat prickles along his neck. *What does she want now?*

"All right?" Leah asks.

"Yes."

"You were late last night. Where were you?"

Simon can't trust his voice to come out right. It might be a squeak, it might be unnaturally deep. Or both at the same time. So he says nothing.

"Where *is* there to go around here?" Leah persists.

Simon shrugs.

"Well?"

"Just out."

"Where are you going now?"

Why does she want to know? What's she playing at? Simon can't imagine why she's speaking to him like this. She's so close up he can smell her hair: a clean, sweet smell. Apples. He's expecting her to laugh at him at any minute.

"Nowhere, really," he says.

"Can I come with you?"

Simon is so shocked he looks directly at her. She's not laughing. Her blue grey eyes stare right back at him.

"Please?" she says, as if she really wants to.

"OK," Simon says, as if he doesn't care either way. "If you really want. I thought I'd just go along the cliff a bit.

There's this place—" he breaks off. *Don't tell her about that! Idiot! It's supposed to be secret.*

"Are you hungry?" Leah asks. "I'm starving. Can we get some chips or something first? I'll buy yours if you want."

He stands behind her, a few paces back, while she orders and pays. She hands him the Styrofoam box and he helps himself to vinegar from the bottle on the food-stand counter. They eat them walking along. It means he doesn't have to speak, although Leah keeps up a steady stream of observations and questions.

"I've seen you out on your bike, and with those boys you hang out with."

"Your mum was pretty mad with you when you got back, wasn't she? She's nice, Nina. And your little sister is really sweet."

It's as if she's been watching him the same as he watches her. He can't quite believe it. He tears the empty chip tray into strips as they walk, then crumples the bits in his hand.

The sky is clearing fast now that the wind's up. Blue sky stretches over the sea, and the sun's almost out. At the end of the town beach they take the concrete path up over the Island. It's concreted over so people in wheelchairs can get up there to see the view from the top over the bay. It's not really an island, of course.

"Let's sit for a bit," Leah says.

Simon perches himself at the other end of the bench. He's hopelessly out of his depth now. What next? He'd been planning to walk along the cliff as far as the rope and the swimming cove, but he can't go there with her.

"Who's your mum's boyfriend, then?"

"She hasn't got one," Simon mumbles.

"Well, who was that guy who drove her home last night?"

"What?"

"Matt someone?"

Simon blushes. "That's just some teacher from my school. Not her boyfriend."

"Oh." Leah smiles.

What does that mean?

And what was my art teacher doing driving Mum home, anyway? She went in her own car. Simon doesn't want to think about any of this.

"I'm going on. See you around." He gets up and starts walking fast up the path to the cliff.

"Hang on. Wait!"

He doesn't. His heart's hammering and he just wants to be by himself. He can hear Leah panting behind. *She doesn't give up easily, does she? She's wearing the wrong things for a rough walk along the cliff. It'll be muddy. Wet grass and gorse brushes your legs all the way along this first bit.* He hears her stumbling along, trying to catch up with him. Eventually he softens, turns, waits.

"I'm not used to going so fast," Leah says, as if she hasn't figured out that he's deliberately trying to leave her behind. "And the path's really slippery."

"You should go back. It gets worse," Simon says.

Below them, the sea crashes and foams on the black rocks. Farther out, it sparkles in sunshine. The path dips and curves along the steep cliff edge. You can get giddy just looking down. He can't get the thought of his mother and Mr. Davies out of his head. *What the hell is she playing at?*

"If you slipped," Leah is saying, "you could fall right

down there onto the rocks. You'd die."

"Possibly," Simon agrees. "But there's bushes and stuff to break your fall."

"Why isn't there a fence? Signs saying how dangerous it is?"

"It's the countryside, isn't it? Anyway, how come you've never been here before? How long've you lived here?"

Leah shrugs. "Years. Always. We don't do walks, my family. We don't do anything for that matter."

They walk in single file along the narrow path. Simon starts thinking back to last night. The dead magpie. Drinking Johnny's hard cider. Nina going on and on at him when he got back so late. He hadn't realized how late it was because of the moonlight.

"Last night," Simon says out loud, "there was this amazing moon. So bright it was like daylight."

"I know," Leah says. "I saw it."

"Everything was silver. The grass, the trees, the sea even."

"Magic," Leah says. "So that's what you were doing last night. Walking."

She still hasn't turned back.

"And other stuff," Simon says. "My friend's got an air rifle."

"Does he kill things?"

"Oh yes. Crows, and a magpie."

"That's unlucky," Leah says. "One for sorrow. What do you kill? With that slingshot thing?"

She *has* been watching.

"Not much," he says. "A rabbit once."

Leah screws up her face, but she doesn't say anything.

Not like Simon expects her to. Like Ellie or Nina, going on about the poor sweet baby bunny. He likes her better for that.

"It's hot now," Leah says. "The path's steaming! Look!"

The air is heavy and full of the stink of wet vegetation. Slightly rotten, with the strong coconut smell of gorse flowers overlaying it.

Simon turns away as Leah tugs her sweatshirt over her head. Not soon enough, though: he can't help glimpsing the taut smooth flesh of her stomach as she pulls up the hem of the sweatshirt. He looks down at the black rocks, the waves crashing in. Feels dizzy.

She follows him along the path, up and down, in and out of each dip and rise of the coastline. He's thirsty, and hot now too. As they scramble up the next hill, he stops to cup his hand in the flow of a tiny spring trickling out of the rock. Leah copies him.

"Is it OK to drink?"

Simon nods. "It's just out of the hillside. Not as if some sheep's been peeing in it or anything, which is what happens in a stream."

Leah leans and stretches herself, hands on her back. "Isn't there a place we can sit? I'm tired."

"Not yet."

He walks the next section of the path more slowly, even though he's not tired at all. It isn't that far now till they reach the place where the path opens out into a steeply sloping green field, and then there's the rope, and a way down. He's going to do it. Take her there. It's too late to turn back now.

8

Leah can't quite believe that she's walked this far and has just virtually rappelled down a rope hanging over a cliff and is still alive. It's taking a summer project she conjured up on a whim to a bit of an extreme, she thinks. When did she last do anything half as active? She hadn't realized Simon was such an outdoors freak. But it's also strangely exhilarating—swinging for a second out over the cliff, before gravity pulls her down and Simon helps her find footholds in the cliffside. And down on the rocks here it's fantastic. The morning's rain has completely cleared away, the wet rocks have dried in the midday sun, and in the shelter of the cliff there's no wind. She rolls up her trousers, slips off her shoes. It's the perfect place for sunbathing. If she can remember the way and steel her nerve for that descent on the rope, she could come here by herself another time and strip right down, tan herself all over.

She watches Simon. He's sitting with his legs dangling over the platform of rock, half turned away, facing a small cove of sparkling sea.

"Is there a way down? A beach?" she asks him.

He shakes his head. "But you can swim off the rocks. It's

hard to get out again, though. The rocks are sharp."

The water looks so inviting. Little waves curl in past the headland into the cove and smooth themselves out over the sandy seabed. A private swimming place. And the rocks to stretch out on and dry afterward.

Eyes closed, Leah imagines she's here with the man from the bookshop. Matt. Being an artist, he's sketching the landscape, and sketching her. Drawings for a future sculpture. He runs his hand over her shoulder to get the feel of the bone, the shape beneath the skin. Her flesh feels as if it's melting under the warmth of his hand. She can feel his breath on her face. Her hair shifts in the breeze, strokes his cheek. He moves closer, leans over her.

"I might swim," Simon says, but he doesn't move.

Leah imagines Matt diving in off the rocks, and her diving after him (somehow, miraculously, she will know how to dive), and her hair streaming out after her like a mermaid.

Leah shivers. A cloud has temporarily covered the sun. She opens her eyes. The rocks look dark. Simon is hunched over, his arms round his knees, staring at the water.

"Well," Leah says. "If you do, I will. When the sun comes back out."

"Will what?"

"Swim. Off the rocks."

"It's freezing," Simon says.

"How do you know?"

"Done it before."

Leah picks her way over the rocks towards him. They are warm to her bare feet. She dips a toe in one of the pools left in a crevice. A tiny fish shoots beneath the weed fringe.

The water's quite warm.

"What about the tides and currents and that?" Leah says. "Is it safe to swim?"

"It's OK if the tide's really low," Simon says. "Like now. You can see the sandy bottom really clearly."

"Go on, then," Leah says.

He looks afraid. It's her, not the sea, that frightens him, she can tell. She backs off slightly.

"You go in and tell me what it's like. I won't watch while you take your things off."

He's obviously not intending to take anything off— only his boots and socks, and maybe his T-shirt. She pretends not to look.

He doesn't dive; he lowers himself, first onto the shelf of rocks below, and then over the edge into the water. She sees him wince as his feet break the surface, hesitate, then he lowers himself right in and his face goes a sort of purple. He gasps, a spontaneous, uncontrolled yelp.

"Cold?" Leah leans over to watch as he starts to swim.

"Freezing!" His voice echoes.

Leah scrambles down to the lower rocks herself. It's cooler already, closer to the water. Maybe she won't swim after all.

Simon has crossed the tiny cove doing the crawl; he now returns on his back and floats a moment, grinning up at her. "Nice once you're in," he lies. "Chicken."

"OK then, I'll show you." Leah steps neatly out of her jeans, folds them, leaves them next to Simon's boots. Her legs are tanned and smooth, warm from the sun. She slips herself over the edge and shrieks at the shock of the water, then starts to swim. It's so cold it hurts. She can't bear it for long. She does her silly, inefficient breaststroke with her head sticking up above the water, around into the shallowest part of the cove and then back, and starts to pull herself out. It isn't that easy. She keeps losing her grip. The waves, even though they are small, push at her, and then the current drags her back. Her legs scrape against the barnacled surface of the rock. Simon swims up behind her to help. She's gasping from the cold, shivering all over. Her fingers are blue white.

"Help me up!" Her teeth chatter.

Simon holds her feet steady and helps shove her up over the ledge. Tiny threads of blood mix with the seawater streaming off her body.

She's trembling all over, and then as the blood starts rushing back into her numb hands and feet it feels as if her whole body's on fire. She starts to laugh.

"Give us a hand, then," Simon shouts up.

She pulls him up and he stands next to her, his clothes plastered to his skinny limbs, a huge wet puddle forming at his feet.

Looking at him makes her laugh more.

He's so helpless, such a drowned rat, standing there with this pathetic look. Leah wriggles into her dry jeans and climbs up a level to a warm sunny spot against the cliff. She'll spare him the misery of peeling off wet clothes in front of her. She quickly takes off her own top and puts on her dry sweatshirt, wrings out the ends of her wet hair, spreads her wet top over the rocks to dry. She feels amazing. It's as if the dip into the sea has brought her back to life. Energy fizzles down her veins. She's actually enjoying herself!

Simon flops next to her. Fully clothed, completely soaked.

Leah squeals. "Get away! You'll make me all wet again!"

He rubs his wet torso with his one dry garment—the T-shirt. "I'll dry in the sun," he explains.

"Take the jeans off at least, Si," Leah tells him. "I can't see anything, not if you've got that huge T-shirt on."

The mood between them has lightened. Simon does a silly sort of dance, one wet foot to the other, flapping at her, and she laughs for real. He turns his back to her to strip off the soaked jeans.

"We'll have to stay here till they dry," he teases.

"What's the time, anyway?"

"No idea."

"I'm supposed to be shopping." Leah giggles.

They both lie there with their eyes shut, and their wet clothes steam in the sun. The sun's high in the sky; it must be early afternoon. Leah's face begins to burn. She moves Simon's boots so they make some shadow for her. She's warmed right through now. Strangely, unexpectedly, she feels completely content. It's been a long time since she's felt this way. High above them, a bird swoops and soars against a blue sky. It calls, a thin high mewing sound.

A slight shift of light and shadow makes her open her eyes. Simon's up; he's wandering over the platform of rocks, searching for something. She watches him: his skinny legs under the long T-shirt, his huge feet, like a puppy with lots of growing still to do. His skin has the faint flush of sunburn which you know will deepen and redden as the day wears on. By nightfall it'll be itchy and unbearable.

9

Simon peers into the rock pool, as if he's searching for creatures, but really he's thinking hard. There's a quick way back home if they cut inland across the fields, but that will mean both arriving home at the same time and some-one might see. If they go back the long way, he'll have to find a way of losing her before they get to the town, but it's easier to do that, and she's already said she's got shopping to do. And it also means she won't know the quick way to the bathing rock. He doesn't want her to come here by her-self. It's his place. Stupid, to have shown her the way down.

But it was amazing, swimming together in the cove. He thinks of that moment, holding her feet so she could climb back out. Her skin.

Behind him her tiny turquoise top is still lying in the sun. When she first got out it was almost see-through, wet against her body.

The mysterious world of the rock pool seems much more knowable to him than Leah. *Leah Sweet.* He says her name in his head twice. *She called me Si. As if we were friends. Are we now?*

There's a buzzard overhead. Gulls below. Tide seems to

be coming back in. They timed their swim perfectly. It will be an hour later tomorrow, to get the right moment. Should he tell her how dangerous it is to swim, unless it's a spring tide? But that will suggest to her that she can come again. Or even come without him.

Too much thinking is making his head hurt. He's too hot again, would love another swim. Needs a drink. He goes dizzy for a moment when he stands up.

"I've got to get back," he says to Leah.

She nods. "How?"

"Same way. Back up with the rope. It's easier going up."

"Wait while I get my top on," Leah says.

She doesn't seem to care whether he sees or not. But he looks away all the same.

When they climb up the cliff he touches her hand. Well, she clings onto him for dear life. It doesn't mean anything. She's scared of falling. They make their way back along the cliff path the way they came, and finally they get back to the Island.

"You're sunburned," Leah says.

"So are you. But you were tan already," Simon stammers. Everything feels different now that they're back.

"I had a really good time," Leah says. "Thanks for letting me tag along."

"You can do your shopping. If it's not too late."

"Yes. Want to come with me?" Leah asks.

"No thanks," Simon says.

"See ya', then!"

Simon waits while she walks slowly down the path towards the town. She doesn't look back. Then he starts off down the hill towards the road. The town beach is packed with people, squeezed into a sandy strip at the top by the encroaching tide. Children bob in the water. The waves drum against the shore. His ears are full of the mesmerizing sound from a whole afternoon of sitting so close to the sea. He buys himself a Coke from the first kiosk he comes to and downs it in one gulp.

The town clock strikes the hour. He counts. Four. He has spent nearly five hours alone with Leah Sweet who is sixteen years old and the most beautiful thing he's ever seen. *Nothing will ever be the same again.*

"Where have you been all day?" Nina asks him the moment he comes through the gate.

"On the beach," Simon tells her. "And I walked along the cliff path a short way."

Nina studies his face. "You've been in the sun too long. Look at you. But hasn't the weather been lovely? I've had a brilliant time too."

"Oh."

"Yes, I met Matt Davies for coffee, and then he gave me a lift out to his place so I could pick up the car, but it was so lovely that we had a little walk around where he lives, and then we had something to eat, and, well—it was lovely."

"Yes. You said."

"What's the matter? Don't you like me having a good time?"

Not with him. He sighs, just so she knows he's fed up with her. "Where's Ellie?" he asks.

"She's been at Rita's all day. She's got her grandchildren staying so she asked Ellie over too, and when it got so sunny they took a picnic down to the beach. And Ellie's just phoned to see if she can sleep over."

"Can she?"

"Yes, of course. What about you? Any plans?"

Simon shakes his head. "I'm going to have a shower."

"OK, love. I'll finish up out here." She waves the garden shears at him. "It looks so much better already, doesn't it?"

It all looks the same to him. Why's she so cheerful suddenly? He kicks his muddy boots off and goes into the kitchen. He cuts a huge slice of bread, loads it with butter, then honey, and shoves the whole thing in his mouth. He pads upstairs to the bathroom.

After his shower, Simon puts on clean boxers and lies on the bed. Dozes. Replays the day, with different versions added in. The window's open. He can hear someone singing. Leah.

He picks up the small book on the bedside table: *The SAS Survival Guide*. He reads the section called "Essentials (Facing Disaster)," and then "Reading the Signs."

He strains to hear the lyrics of the song that's drifting in through the window. His face and arms are glowing from the day's sun.

The phone rings.

"For you," Nina calls up the stairs.

Simon bounces down, two stairs at a time. Nina's still hovering in the kitchen doorway so he turns his back on her.

"Hi," he says into the phone.

"Want to come out tonight? Go hunting again? Dan's allowed out. We can get some cans."

Simon feels a stab of disappointment. It's Johnny. He'd expected—who?

"Si? Are you still there? Well? About eight? No point in going earlier. The rabbits don't come out till it's dusk. Bring your slingshot, yes, and some ammo? Dan and I'll come for you."

"OK." He puts the phone back.

Nina reappears from the kitchen. "Well?"

"What?"

"What did he want? Are you going out?"

Simon frowns. "Yes. So?"

"Well, it's helpful to know, so I can make my own plans. I might invite someone around."

"With me safely out of the way, you mean."

"Probably not at all safely!" Nina laughs.

She's refusing to get wound up by him. Won't notice his sarcastic tone.

"So get yourself something to eat, Si. I'll eat later."

Back upstairs, the singing has stopped. Simon picks up his book again and reads through the advice on finding your way at night: "Using the Moon for a Rough East-West Reference," "Using the Stars for Navigation."

He starts thinking about Dan and Johnny and him. He might as well make the most of it. Why don't they take a tent? Stay out all night? Or, even better, make their own shelter for the night? He looks up the section in the survival book and then goes back downstairs to phone Johnny. He won't tell Nina till he's gotten it all planned and the other parents have agreed, and then she won't be able to say no. She'll have made her own arrangements for the evening by then anyway. He won't think about that.

"We'll make a fire and cook rabbit, if we get any, and let's take marshmallows, and I've made some of that dough stuff to cook on sticks."

Dan and Johnny wait in the kitchen while Simon packs his backpack with mess kits, and two different sorts of knife, and his survival fuel stove for emergencies, and matches, and his army surplus water bottle. He retrieves the dough, wrapped in a plastic bag, from the fridge, and three packets of marshmallows from the top cupboard.

Nina comes in from the garden. "So, where's your tent? And sleeping bags?"

Dan answers her. "We're gonna make a group shelter with a tarp. And it's too hot for sleeping bags."

"Hmm."

Johnny chips in. "It'll be fine, honest. We've got a groundsheet. We can shove bracken underneath for insulation."

"In any case," Simon says, "we're only going to be over in the fields. We can just come home if we're cold."

"You will be really careful, won't you, of the cliffs in the dark? No swimming off the rocks, either, or anything else foolhardy."

Johnny and Dan will take that out on him later.

He doesn't turn back to wave or anything, although he knows his mother's there at the gate, watching them go. He's vaguely aware of someone at the window in the house opposite too. He doesn't look up. As soon as they leave the road and take the footpath over the fields he eases up. It's going to be a good night, after all. The air's still warm even though it's after eight. Long shadows stretch over the hay-field. They'll choose a place to rig up the shelter first, and get wood for a fire, and then they can start hunting.

10

Sparks from the fire float up into the night sky.
Simon's still hungry; they haven't caught any meat and the
dough sticks don't fill you up, and the marshmallows have
started to make him feel sick. He lets one drop into the fire
on purpose, watches the sticky goo melt, blacken, and crisp
on the logs. He's the only one in a fit-enough state to keep
the fire going, feeding it with more wood. They've finished
all the beer. Johnny and Dan seem to find everything incredibly funny. They've been telling each other ridiculous
stories.

"And then there's this boy," Dan goes on. "This is true,
right? About fifteen years old. They found his body lying
on the path near the big standing stone on the moor. Stone
cold dead. Like some sort of human sacrifice, only no one
ever found out *what* had killed him. No marks on him, no
reason at all. It was as if he'd died of fright. And on moon-
lit nights, his ghost can still be seen, making its spooky way
along the field path to the ancient stone."

"Whooooo!" Johnny warbles, in a mock ghostly voice.
"And if you see him, you know you're next."

"... But the scariest of all is the living, not the dead.

Scariest of all is *Mad Ed*." Dan lowers his voice to a dramatic hiss. "Armed with a loaded shotgun, patrolling his land, searching out enemy snipers. Mad Ed, who doesn't understand the war is over. Who plays it out in his mind over and over, the scene where his brother got shot and he didn't. Waiting to get his revenge."

"What do you mean, revenge?" Simon asks. "You're kidding, right?"

Dan shakes his head slowly from side to side, for effect. "For real."

"I thought you said—" Simon looks at Johnny. "Well, that's not what you told me before. You said about his dad having shell shock. Nerve-gas poisoning or something. And that Mad Ed was a loner, a bit weird. You didn't say he was out looking for revenge . . . thinking he's still fighting some war . . . "

Johnny glances back at Dan. "Well, whatever. Anyway, *scar-y!*" He laughs.

"It's not funny," Simon says. "It's serious. I mean, if he's got a gun, and we're out here—and it's his land . . . is it his land?"

Both Johnny and Dan shrug. "Lighten up, Si. We're just giving you shit."

Now Simon can't be sure. Both Dan and Johnny are too drunk for him to be able to trust anything either says. He's starting to feel really spooked. He knows they were kidding around earlier, but he's seen that guy with his own eyes. Seen the gun. It isn't funny.

"Perhaps we should go back?"

"No way!"

"I'm serious. What if he finds us when we're asleep and

thinks we're the enemy, and shoots us? Think about it."

"It's dark. It's nearly midnight. No one is going to be snooping around this time of night. Anyway, we were just kidding."

Simon doesn't like it. He's the outsider again. The joke's at his expense.

Dan seems to have collapsed on the grass, still laughing. Johnny's pissing into the hedge.

Simon moves away from the firelight. He can see the stars that much better now. Hundreds and thousands of them. Billions. Light shining from way back in time. Light from stars that aren't even there any more.

Dan's virtually asleep, and Johnny's stirring up the embers of the fire with one of the arrows he whittled earlier. They're going to put flights on the end when they can get some big enough feathers. Goose feathers are best, but seagulls' will do. Or magpies'. It's called fletching. Johnny's designed (but not yet made) his own crossbow; they cost more than seventy quid if you buy them over the Internet. Simon's not sure they're even legal. In the meantime, the arrows can be shot with their slingshots. With a metal tip they'd be deadly.

There's no way Simon can sleep yet. His head's too full of wild imaginings, his own and Dan's. "I'm going for a walk," he says aloud.

No one answers.

Simon walks slowly away from the encampment, climbs the wall into the next field to get back on the footpath. The moon's risen above the horizon, huge and silver. It lights the way. When he looks back, he can see no trace of the camp, or the fire. Perhaps it's safe after all. No one could know they were there, sleeping under the tarpaulin cover. Not until they were right close up.

Simon takes his slingshot out of his pocket and loads it up with a stone from the wall. Just a stone.

His heart stops thudding so hard after he's crossed two fields, two stiles. It's so still he can hear the sound of the sea crashing over the rocks even though it must be half a mile to the cliff from here. His boots are damp from the dew; he's leaving a trail of silvered footsteps in the grass. Some small creature scurries and scratches along the wall near the next stile; he waits and watches.

Out of the corner of his eye he glimpses something else moving, pale and ghostly in the moonlight. It's coming right at him. He turns, gives a strangled squeal and finds himself face to face with an owl. For a brief moment they stare into each other's eyes: two creatures of the night, on equal terms. It's a moment of recognition. *You too? Hunting?* Then the owl floats silently on, its white wings stretched out, its claws curved ready for the kill.

Wow! He wishes there was someone with him now, someone to feel it too. He imagines telling Leah. *There it was, a barn owl. Looking at me right in the eye. With its huge dark eyes in a heart-shaped face, this close.* He'll hold out his arms to show her how close. And then she'll do the same, like the owl. Look at him that close. And . . . and . . .

He almost trips. A rock jutting out of the path. He's been lost in thought, hasn't noticed how the path's changing. More stones, and instead of rough field grass either side it's short grass, like a lawn. There's a building of some sort.

As he gets closer he can see huge stones, but it's not a house, or a barn even. The stone slabs are roofed with turf;

it's a burial chamber, a long barrow.

It's just some old monument, there's nothing to worry about. You get them all over the place, this part of the country. So why does he just stand there? Those stupid stories Dan was telling. The dead who come back to haunt the living. The restless dead, whose spirits inhabit the land. But it's more than that. He's felt it before, the strange sensation that somehow the past isn't past, but still going on. People and events trapped in the places where they happened, like fossils in rocks, except there's nothing to see with your eyes. You just feel it. If you really pay attention.

It's so very still and silent. As if any noise is sucked up and absorbed in the deep stone chambers, muffled by the still-growing turf roof. Simon dares himself closer. He treads softly between the two outer stones of the entrance tunnel, takes a last look at the star-studded sky and ducks in under the huge lintel stone of the first chamber.

There's a different quality to the darkness inside. It's thick and soft. It pulls him in deeper.

From the main chamber, a sort of corridor, smaller ones branch off. He creeps through one of the low doorways and crouches in the space, and suddenly he hears a new sound, like a whisper echoing around, a sound that might be in his head, or might be in the chambers, like the murmur of sea in a shell that is only the sound of your own blood in your ears. It seems to get louder. He puts his hands over his ears to see what happens. It muffles the whisper. So it must be coming from outside himself. He leans over and lays his ear against the stone walls. They are warm. It's like being inside the body of a stone creature, living and breathing. The stones have a voice of their own, and a language he doesn't understand. He starts to feel dizzy. He dips his head back out through the doorway, takes a breath, but there's no more air in the central chamber either. He can feel a sort of pressure on his lungs. It's so dark he can't make out his own hand right in front of his face, as if someone has blocked up the entrance and shut out the moonlight. He can't see which way to go, which way takes him out, which takes him farther, deeper into the hollow chamber. He starts to sweat; it prickles along his neck and his forehead. His hands are clammy. The noise seems louder still. And then he blacks out.

11

When he wakes up, he finds himself lying just outside the burial mound, on damp grass. He lies there with his eyes open, trying to make sense of what has happened and work out how he got here, like this. Above him, the huge sky is ablaze with stars, more than he can ever remember seeing before. He starts to make out the patterns he knows: the seven stars of the Big Dipper; Cassiopeia; Orion the hunter.

His head aches as if he's knocked it really hard. Or something hit him. His hand feels the place. There's a bump, big as an egg.

What happened?

His legs are stiff, and his sweatshirt is damp from dew. He sits up and automatically feels for the slingshot in his jeans pocket. Not there. He stands up, searches the grass. It must have fallen out when he was in the stone chamber. But he's not going back in there. No way.

The moon has moved into quite a different part of the sky, so hours must have passed with him lying out stone cold. Why has no one come to find him?

He's suddenly freezing cold. The entrance to the burial chamber looks like a huge dark mouth. He can't imagine

what made him want to go inside it, before. *Before what?*
What exactly happened in there? He starts to shake violently.

A wind has started up. It makes a low moaning sound
as it whistles through the grass, through the dry bracken
and low heather. He can hear the sea thundering on the
rocks below. It sounds so close now.

He's got to get back, find the others, check that they're
all right. Walking without the slingshot in his hand, Simon
feels vulnerable and small. Every sound makes him start.
He retraces his steps. Starts thinking back to Dan's stories.
What would he do if he met that crazy guy here, now? He's
defenseless. He looks around for something that might
make a sort of weapon: a stick at least, or a stone. There
aren't any decent trees, though, just thin, windblown thorn
bushes, and the only rocks are wedged deep in the earth,
part of the land itself. So he walks quietly, every sense alert,
ready to hide, or run. What if Mad Ed has already come
across the sleeping figures of Johnny and Dan? They'd have
been too drunk to defend themselves. Whose stupid idea
was this, anyway, to camp overnight?

He's almost there now. There's the faintest flush of light
in the east. Dawn. It lifts his spirits to see the light beginning to spread out across the sky. Everything changes; the
dark shadows pale to fuzzy grey. Nothing looks quite so
scary. A low mist rolls along the grass like something on a
film set. He crosses the last field towards the stile. And
then stops. There, neatly laid out on the top of the stile, is
his slingshot and five small stones arranged in a circle.

He swings around, searching for someone lurking in the
hedgerow, watching him, lining up the sights on a gun, getting him into focus. But there's nothing to see, just the grey

shapes of a thorn bush, the stone walls, the damp grass ruf-fled by the wind that's blowing in off the sea. He grabs the slingshot and scatters the stones, even though they are the perfect size for ammunition, climbs the stile and runs to-wards the camp where he left Johnny and Dan.

His breath rasps in his throat. His chest feels tight again, like it did in the burial chamber, as if there's not enough air, only that can't be true here. If anything, there's too much.

He sees the dark green tarpaulin strung between two thorn trees, and then at last makes out the two huddled shapes beneath.

"Johnny?" Simon pushes the inert figure with his boot toe. "Wake up."

His throat feels tight. He kicks him again, more insis-tently.

Johnny's in such a heavy sleep he doesn't even stir. Simon crouches closer. Now he can see Johnny's face. In the pale light of dawn it's ashen. Sudden terror clutches Simon all over again. What if he's not asleep, but . . . ?

He prods the shoulder nearest him, half expecting the body to roll over, to reveal a bloody, gaping wound.

There's a groan and then Johnny opens one eye.

"What?"

"You've got to wake up."

"What? It's still dark. We've only just got to sleep. Where the hell've you been?"

"I went for a walk—I told you—but something hap-pened—"

Johnny rolls back over and buries his head in his hood. His voice is muffled. "Yeah. Right. Wait till morning, OK?

Some of us need sleep."

Simon rocks back on his heels. He looks across at Dan, slumped over and breathing noisily through his mouth. What's the point? But he's so far from sleep himself now. It's too lonely, awake by himself. Or worse, awake with some-one else, someone unseen, watching him. He takes the slingshot out of his pocket again and examines it more closely. It's definitely his, worn in the same places, the same make. And he definitely had it with him when he was walking along the path towards the burial chamber. So un-less he dropped it earlier, and Johnny or Dan found it when they were searching for him (did they? In the state they were in?) someone else must have. Someone out walking in the middle of the night.

He shivers. The fire's out. He tries blowing on the ashes to raise a spark, but the fire's dead. He scurries around for a while, gathering up twigs and dry lichen for kindling, and some bigger sticks to burn. There isn't much, and it's all a bit damp from the dew. He concentrates on getting a spark with the flint striker, and then carefully feeds and shelters the tiny flame until the twigs catch light. A thin spiral of white smoke rises and he hears the first shift and rustle of fire. He's done it. He warms his hands and face.

Once it's going properly he can relax a bit, but that means his mind's free to think. It keeps returning to the slingshot in his pocket. A hand reaching in, pulling it out, while he lay unconscious on the ground. Was he uncon-scious? Did he knock his head on the stone lintel when he was clambering out? Or did someone do that too? And then they left a trail of evidence to spook him more? But why would anyone do that? And the neat circle of stones, laid out like a present? None of it makes sense.

The fire begins to crackle and spit. The damp wood makes too much smoke. Dan coughs, grunts, turns over. Simon seizes his chance.

"Oi, Dan! Wake up!"

"Whazz it?"

"Wake up. Properly. Listen."

One eye opens warily. He groans again. "Head!"

"Drink some water. Sit up. I'll get some." Simon rummages for a water bottle in the muddle of supplies at one end of the tarpaulin shelter. "Here."

"What's up?" Dan's speech is still slurred. "What happened?"

"I don't know, that's the point. Something really weird. I mean *seriously* weird."

Dan's in danger of falling asleep again unless Simon makes it quick and exciting.

"I nearly died."

Dan eyes him suspiciously. "What d'ya mean?"

"I went for a walk and found this stone burial place, and then someone knocked me unconscious. And stole my slingshot."

"Good try," Dan says, "but not plausible enough. Not in the sober light of morning. Very . . . early . . . morning," he says slowly, to make the point.

"I'm not making this up, Dan. It's for real. I woke up on the ground and my head hurt, as if I'd been hit with something, and my slingshot had gone."

"What's that, then?" Dan points to the slingshot in Simon's hand.

"Well that's even more weird. 'Cos someone had put it

back on the stile, obviously for me to find."

Dan shakes his head. "Sad. Get some sleep. You'll feel better in the morning."

It does sound feeble, said out loud. No wonder Dan's not interested. Simon turns his back on the fire to warm it up a bit.

The light's spreading in the sky, turning it golden. Perhaps he'll make a hot drink. He rummages in his backpack and fishes out two packets of tomato soup, pours water into a pan and balances it on two flat stones over the fire. Johnny and Dan sleep on. He feels utterly alone. His head still aches.

He thinks briefly of Nina, wonders whether she went out with Matt Davies last night. He's not that bad, not really. It's just . . . well, Nina's his mum, isn't she? Then he starts thinking about Leah. He imagines telling her what's happened. She'd listen, and her eyes would go even bigger and rounder, and maybe she'd giggle a bit, and she'd think it was really scary. Maybe she'd say something like "Let's go back there together, to the burial chamber, and see what we can find." And once they were inside, she'd grab his hand and they would be standing really close to each other and then . . .

A sudden gust of wind channels smoke right into his face. He coughs and stumbles up, away from the smoke, and knocks the pan over on to the grass.

"Damn!"

As he bends to pick it up, something makes him look round. A tiny noise, or just some intangible change in the air alerts him. Someone's there. He knows they are. Watching him.

12

Simon freezes.

He scans the ground for stones the right size for ammo.
There's one near the fire. Very carefully, he stretches out
one foot to nudge it close enough to pick up. Silently, he
loads the slingshot. His heart's thudding again. Dan and
Johnny sleep on, unaware. *How vulnerable they are*, Simon
thinks. *How stupid. They should have thought before about
keeping a night watch, doing shifts.* Simon edges himself
round. He's armed, ready. He waits. Nothing.

The newly risen sun is flooding the fields with golden
light. It's breathtakingly beautiful. But something's there,
he's sure of it. All the tiny hairs on his arms and the back
of his neck are standing upright. Alongside the stone wall,
there's deep shadow where someone could be hiding. He
can't see from here.

Another sudden movement. He swings round, ready to
fire. Three small rabbits bound out from the shadow, race
round, then settle to graze. Simon almost laughs aloud with
the release in tension. Was that all it was? He waits. He
could easily get the rabbits. They could have them for
breakfast, spit-roasted over the fire. But he doesn't even try.

For one moment, he'd identified with the rabbits; they're on the same side.

Just as he gives up and sits back on the ground near the fire, a shot cracks out. One rabbit keels over, the others race back to the wall.

"Whazzat?" Dan sits up, rubbing his head. Johnny's woken too.

"Sshh," Simon whispers.

"Who is it?"

"Can't see. Get your ammo ready."

"Hang on," Dan says. "You crazy or what?"

"Sshh," Simon says. "It's that crazy guy. For real."

"He's just potting rabbits," Johnny says. "Cool it, Si."

"He's got a gun," Simon says, "and he's been watching us. Who knows what he'll do next?"

Dan gives a very loud and dramatic yawn.

"I'm serious," Simon hisses. "Idiot."

Johnny half laughs. "What are you going to do? Shoot him with a slingshot?"

Dan does an impression of someone getting shot in the head. He writhes in agony and collapses on the ground with his tongue hanging out. Johnny starts to laugh again, but stops mid-laugh and looks nervously at Simon. "What was that?"

They listen. It comes again, a dragging sound.

Johnny grabs at Dan. "Shut it. Listen."

Fear is contagious.

"Get ready," Simon says in a low voice. "Load your air rifle." He holds his slingshot taut, aimed at a patch of wall, beyond which the noise has stopped. One stone might not be enough and he can hear Johnny fumbling with the tin

of pellets, trying to load the air rifle with shaking hands.
He's imagined the scene often enough. Now it's for real.

"Perhaps we shouldn't . . ." Dan starts to say.

"Shut up!" Simon hisses. "Ready?" He glances briefly
behind him towards Johnny, who holds the air rifle to his
shoulder, eyes trained along the barrel. He hears the safety
catch click off. This is it. There's a sudden crack of shot firing out, and then another, and Simon feels the slingshot
twang as his stone flies through the air. Someone yells out,
though in the muddle Simon can't tell who. He moves
stealthily, like a trained soldier, into position next to the
wall and then slowly raises himself up so he can see over
the top. A man is bending over a dead rabbit, picks it up,
holds it by the ears so that the limp body dangles down and
bumps his leg as he walks away over the field towards the
next stile. His boots leave a line of flattened, damp grass
spotted with blood.

Simon's heart is still thumping manically. He turns to
look at Johnny. He has lowered his air rifle, looks dazed.
Dan's huddled over on the grass, rocking slightly, his hands
over his ears.

"What happened?" Simon asks.

"I don't know! When I heard the shot I just panicked
and fired." Johnny joins Simon at the wall, looking over at
the figure disappearing from view. "Who was it? Did you
see?"

"That guy. I told you! Shot the rabbit deliberately to
scare us off. Make sure we knew he had a gun. Really dangerous. So close. Stupid idiot. Nearly got himself shot.
Serves him right." Simon's hands are trembling.

A funny whimpering sound is coming from Dan. He's

still rocking back and forth.

"What's wrong with him?" Simon asks Johnny. They watch him for a moment. From behind Dan's hand comes a thin trickle of blood.

"Christ!" Simon says. "You shot him!"

He goes over to Dan to look. Peels his hand away from his head. There's lots of blood. Thick, dark, oozing. Dan's shut his eyes. He groans.

"How bad is it?" Johnny kneels down next to him. "How the hell did that happen? It can't have been me, he was behind me. Must have been that crazy guy after all. You were right."

"It's bad enough," Simon says. "Not fatal." He bites his lip. He's seen the wound. But it's not from an air-rifle pellet. It has the jagged edges made by a stone. Shot at close range by a slingshot. *Shit!*

"What'll we do?" Johnny asks.

"Get him home. My house is nearest. Pack up the stuff and come back for it later. We might have to carry him."

They survey Dan's lanky body.

"We need to stop the blood, don't we?" Johnny says. "Pressure on the wound. What can we use?" He ransacks his own bag, then Dan's and Simon's, searching for something to tie round his head. In the end they tear a T-shirt into strips and it seems to work, sort of. Dan whimpers all the time they're doing it, like a wounded dog. Simon feels sick.

"I saw this program," Simon says, "where they turned the tarpaulin into a stretcher. I'll see if I can work out how to do it."

"Can't he walk?"

"I don't know. The wound's deep. He might faint or something."

"Why don't you run back and get someone? What time is it?"

"Dunno. Early. You stay here with him, then? What if that guy comes back?"

Dan's stopped moaning. He opens his eyes and stares at them.

"You OK, man? What happened?" Johnny says. "It wasn't me, was it? Shot you?"

Dan grimaces. "It was a bloody stone. From your sling-shot, you moron, Piper."

Johnny stares at Simon, openmouthed.

"I—I don't know how . . . the slingshot went off just like that . . . I didn't see where the stone went . . . it must have bounced off the wall or something—"

"Does it hurt a lot?" Johnny's staring at the blood seeping through the T-shirt.

"Too bloody right it does. Now I've got a headache on top of the hangover I already had."

Simon kicks out the fire. He scatters the ashes. He bundles the pans into his backpack along with everything else.

"What're you doing, man?" Dan asks.

"We've got to get back. Take care of your head. It looks bad. Do you reckon you can walk?"

Dan nods. "Ouch. Hurts when I move it."

"We'll go really slow."

They eventually make their way across the fields, stile to stile in a diagonal line all the way back to the lane. Blood begins to drip through the strips of cloth. It's a relief to get to the road and to see the house. The curtains are still drawn shut.

Not at Leah's house, though. She doesn't miss a thing, does she? She's standing at her window, practically naked, watching their slow progress up the road. She gives Simon a half smile, flutters her hand.

"Slut," says Johnny. "Who does she think she's waving at?"

Simon prays that she doesn't open the window wider, or call something out to him. He keeps his eyes down and one arm supporting Dan's shoulders. Dan's face is completely drained of color.

They stumble through the unlocked back door. Dan slumps onto a kitchen chair.

Voices drift down from upstairs. Two voices. Nina and a man.

13

"Si? What's going on? It's so early! Is everything all right?"

From the foot of the stairs, Simon can see Nina at her bedroom door, hastily tying her bathrobe around herself. He beckons her down. "Dan's hurt his head."

"How bad?" She nearly slips in her rush down the bare stairs. "Where is he?" Her voice sounds shaky.

"Here. In the kitchen. It's OK, he walked back, it's not too bad. Just bleeding a lot."

Simon flinches as she bends over Dan, inspects the bloodied cotton strips.

Nina frowns. "Poor you, Dan. We need to get these off and have a proper look."

Dan groans.

"How much does it hurt? Can you bear it if I take these off?"

Dan nods stoically.

Simon has to look away when she peels back the strips, but he hears Nina's sharp intake of breath.

"What happened?" she asks Dan gently.

"A stone. An accident," Dan says.

Johnny looks at Simon, grins. Simon's shaking. Can't stop.

Nina purses up her lips. "Hospital job, I'm afraid. You'll need stitches and a proper clean up. I'll get dressed and then I can take you. Phone Dan's mother, Si."

"*No!*" Dan's voice is surprisingly panicked. "Don't. I mean, she'll worry too much. Please. They'll still be asleep."

Nina looks severe. "*I'd* want to know, if I were her."

"But you're not," Simon says.

"Simon!"

They all look up. Footsteps are coming slowly down the stairs.

Oh no! Simon thinks, *Please no.*

Too late. A familiar voice rings out. "Everything OK, Nina?"

Mr. Davies, art teacher, walks into the kitchen. He pauses. "Ah."

Stunned silence.

Someone coughs. Simon knows Johnny and Dan are staring at him. He won't look. *As if things weren't bad enough already!*

"I need to get Dan to the hospital," Nina says.

"What's happened, Dan?" Mr. Davies peers at the bloody wound. He rests his hand briefly on Dan's shoulder. "Ouch. Looks nasty. How did it happen, Dan?"

Nina gives him one of her looks.

"Shall I take him in?" Mr. Davies offers.

"No, I'll do it. You could stay here with the boys, if you want. I think you all know each other already." She grins, sheepish.

How could she? "We don't need looking after," Simon mutters.

"Don't be rude," Nina says. "The evidence goes against you, I'm afraid. Look at Dan."

She looks sad. They've ruined her morning, of course. She wasn't planning on them coming back while *he* was still here.

"We could come to the hospital," Simon suggests. "Johnny and me. Dan?"

Dan shrugs. "If you want."

"No," Nina says. "Absolutely not. You two stay here. You've already caused enough trouble."

"What!" Simon's indignant.

"Don't think I don't know! It was that bloody slingshot, wasn't it?"

"No," Johnny and Dan both say too quickly. But Nina's not listening anyway. She's running upstairs to get dressed, while Mr. Davies holds a pad of gauze he's found in the first-aid box to Dan's head, telling him to relax.

Johnny's looking at Simon in a very strange way.

"What's he doing here?" he asks at the first opportunity, when Mr. Davies goes upstairs to say something to Nina.

Simon looks at his feet helplessly.

"Your mum, screwing a teacher!"

"Shut up!" Simon says. It's all a complete nightmare.

"I'll make us all a cup of tea," Mr. Davies says, coming back in and filling the kettle, just as if he lives there all the time. *Bloody nerve.* "Except you, Dan. In case you need an anesthetic. Sorry."

Simon shakes his head in disbelief. He lopes out into the garden. Johnny follows him. They lean against the back wall. Neither speaks for a while. Simon's headache's worse.

Nina appears, maneuvers Dan into the front seat of the car, then goes back to speak to Mr. Davies and finally gets into the car herself. She winds down the window.

"You stay right here till I get back, Simon. Don't go anywhere, understand? And the least you can do is be polite to Matt while he's here. He's not staying after all. You just keep out of trouble till I'm back, OK?"

Dan does a V-sign at them through the window as the car pulls away.

"Your mum's pretty stressed out!" Johnny says.

Simon feels suddenly angry, defensive. He doesn't like anyone else to criticize her, even if he does. "She just worries," he says. "She does it for two, since my dad died."

That shuts Johnny up all right.

"Think I'll head home," Johnny says after a while. "Crash for a bit. We can get the gear later."

"Yeah. Right."

"Give us a call later?"

"OK."

"If she lets you."

Simon scowls. They stand facing each other, silent.

"You could have said it was your stone that did it, when you first saw. Why did you let me think I did it?" Johnny asks eventually.

"I don't know." Simon's voice comes out small and pathetic. "I got scared."

"Me too. But he'll be all right?" Johnny adds after a while. "Won't he?"

Simon nods. "Luckily. But it was close too close. Did

you see? Just an inch either way and it might have been different. I could've killed him, Johnny."

"Nah. Not with a slingshot. Now, with an air rifle at that range . . . makes you think!"

They both look serious for a bit, as if they feel they ought to, then Simon starts to laugh, and Johnny joins in, and once they've started neither of them can stop, so that they're doubled over with laughter when Matt comes out to see what's going on.

"What's the joke?" he asks.

They're still too paralyzed with laughter to be able to speak.

He gives up. "Tea's inside. Tell Nina I'll give her a call later. I'm off. Sure you'll be OK?"

Johnny and Simon look at each other again and that sparks them off even more. They're still laughing when Matt Davies drives off.

"I'm starving," Simon says finally.

"Me too."

"Let's have a big fry-up."

They raid the fridge for bacon and eggs. Then they find croissants in the bread box as well, and a new jar of apricot jam, some expensive brand, and a bowl of strawberries on the dresser. As if Nina's planned a special breakfast just for them.

It dawns on Simon who the special breakfast was really for.

"Should we eat all this?" Johnny asks. "Won't your mum mind?"

"No," Simon says. "She's nice like that."

It gives him enormous pleasure to devour it all, so that

even if Matt Davies does happen to return when Nina gets back from the hospital, there'll be absolutely nothing left. Serves them right.

How could she? With Mr. Davies? And secretly, when I was away, and she thought I wouldn't find out. Because she knew how much I'd mind.

Once Johnny's gone home, Simon goes upstairs for a shower and then crashes on his bed. It's deliciously soft. His head still aches. He can feel a sort of egg on the top. *I must have bashed it on the stones at the burial chamber when I was coming out. Mustn't I? What happened, really?* He might find out something about those chambers sometime. How old they are. Who they were for. Go back for another look, with a flashlight next time. Might ask Leah. Might not.

She's singing along to the radio over at her house; she must know he can hear. They've both got their windows open. He lies there for a while, listening, then he can't help himself. He goes and stands at the window. She's already there, waiting for him.

She mouths something at him, but he can't make out what. She indicates to him to go downstairs, and by the time he's gotten to the bottom she's standing at the open back door.

"Everyone out? You all alone?" she asks.

He nods, speechless.

"Can I come in, then?"

He nods again. *Like a bloody puppet.*

"What for?" he blurts out.

"Oh, Simon," she says in her syrupy voice. "To see you, of course. Find out what's been going on this morning. Like

118

Piccadilly Circus at your house, all the comings and goings!"

Another stupid nod. *What's wrong with him?*

"Shall we go up to your room?" she asks, her eyes all round and innocent.

"O-O-OK," he splutters. He's never had a girl in his room before. Apart from Ellie, of course.

His hands feel too big and he trips over his own feet. There's nowhere proper to sit, so when she plumps herself down on the bed he backs himself up against the table.

She pats the bed next to her. "I won't bite, promise!"

He's so intent on not touching her that he doesn't hear anything she says. Then he hears a car engine slowing outside, and he shoots up from the bed.

"You'll have to go," he says. "Quick."

"What's the matter with you? Why are you so jumpy?"

"Mum's back from the hospital. Hurry up!"

"So? I'll tell Nina I came to see Ellie, if you're so worried. Where is Ellie anyway?"

"Sleeping over. Rita's."

Leah gets up, tantalizingly slowly, and slouches downstairs. It's unbearable. Simon stands in his room, head in his hands. He can hear everything, nonetheless.

"Hi, Nina. I just came by to see Ellie, but Simon says she's not here. How are you? Enjoy your meal last night?"

"Yes thanks, Leah. Ellie'll be back later this morning. Will you be free to babysit again sometime soon?"

"Anytime! Just say when. Say hi to Ellie for me. Bye."

Once she's gone, Simon cranes down from the top of the stairs. "What happened?" he asks Nina.

"Let me make coffee, and then I'll tell you. Come down and sit with me, Si."

He walks slowly downstairs, trying to guess her mood. He watches her pour water into the French press cof- feemaker. He likes to push the plunger down. If you do it really quickly, it bubbles up and splurges all over the table. But not today. Not such a good idea.

"I don't know why Dan was going on like that about his mother," she says. "She seemed very nice when I took him back just now. Not at all angry."

"That's because you were there, of course," Simon says. "Anyway, what did the hospital say?"

"We didn't have to wait long. There was only one other person. They cleaned him up, and it didn't look so bad then. There's always loads of blood with a head wound, ap- parently. Then they glued it together. That's what they do these days, not stitches. And he has to be a bit careful not to get it wet, and they gave him a tetanus shot, but basi- cally he's fine. Very lucky. You too."

He shifts uneasily as she peers at him over her coffee cup. "So now tell me what really happened."

"I don't know. Honest."

Nina sighs.

He stares at the table. "We were messing around. I let the slingshot go without meaning to, and it was loaded with a small stone, and I think it must have bounced off one of those drystone walls and hit Dan. It could've hap- pened to anyone."

Nina sighs more heavily. "The *whole* story, Simon."

"Well, we got a bit spooked. There was this man delib- erately scaring us, shooting his gun very early this morn- ing—"

"What sort of man? What do you mean, shooting?"

"That crazy guy everyone knows round here. Mad Ed. He's got a gun."

"For rabbits, rats. Not that I approve, of course. He's not *mad*, Simon. And it's not a very nice way of talking about someone either. Calling him that."

"It's what everyone calls him!"

"Well, I don't like it. Just call him Ed. He's a bit strange, maybe, but he's hardly dangerous!"

"How do you know? He was doing it on purpose, scaring us. He doesn't like people on his land and he thinks the war's still on and we had to fire in self-defense."

"You did what? I don't believe I'm hearing this! Silly stories about the war . . . Honestly, Simon!"

"You said you wanted to know!"

"I did."

Simon fiddles with the cutlery left lying on the table. The knife spins round beautifully if you set it going just right.

Nina's going off at some tangent now about people who are a bit different and not branding them with labels like "mad." He half listens to her story about a man with shell-shock who lived in her village when she was little and the children made up stories about him and of course none of it was true. "He was harmless," she says, "and very lonely. People used to run away from him."

She's gone way off the subject now. The big lecture about weapons and accidents hasn't happened. He drifts off. He hardly got any sleep last night.

He jolts awake again and catches the tail end of a sentence. ". . . And you could've left me a croissant at least. You're so selfish sometimes."

"Sorry." He puts on his little boy voice. "Sorry, Mummy!" It usually makes her laugh. Not today.

"Wash up the breakfast things, please, and then clear up the camping gear."

"We left most of it in the field. I'll have to go back for it. I'm really tired. Can't I sleep first?"

"As long as you don't forget later. And you can pick up Ellie for me from Rita's. Since you've completely wrecked my morning." She pauses on the threshold, on her way out into the garden.

"I'm sorry if you were a bit taken aback to find Matt here. I hadn't planned it like that."

Obviously.

"It's just—well, I do like him, but it's early days, OK? So I don't want to get all heavy about it. It's new for me too, having a *man*friend. . . . You can cope with that, can't you? You're old enough to understand. Now I'm going to do some gardening."

Simon lies on his bed, trying not to think about what Nina has just said. He leafs through *Air Gun Weekly*. He skip-reads an article on roost-shooting crows, then scans the swap shop section for bargains. He could get himself an air rifle for less than two hundred pounds. Where could he keep it, so Nina doesn't find out? She'll never agree to him having one, especially now this has happened with the slingshot. She always overreacts. Sees the dangers in everything. She doesn't understand about taking risks and living on the edge a bit. She wants everything too safe. He doesn't want to live like that. He wishes he were older. And that Dad...but what's the point in that?

He dozes on the bed. Sun floods in through the open window. He can hear blunt shears tearing long grass as Nina works her way around between the plum trees in the garden. She's got the radio on in the kitchen. *Mum and Matt Davies. Together. In her bed. Doing it. No. Don't think of it.*

He flips through the magazine pages again, examines the millions of advertisements for different weapons. There's an article about game-keeping.

He must have been about six or seven. Dad and he were playing a game in the woods. It must have been autumn: the bracken was all red, with black stalks. Trees golden. Leaves falling. He was running, sliding in the mud, his senses alert, looking out for a place to hide so he could jump out on Dad and make him squeal and then Simon would laugh and laugh. That was the game they always played.

He was way ahead. The path forked. Which way? He chose the right fork, and ran on. Suddenly the trees were spaced out more, there was more grey sky and long wet grass underfoot, and everything felt different. Odd. He stopped. Instead of birdsong and the rustling of leaves there was a weird silence. And a smell. Not the normal earthy, damp-leaves smell, but a foul stink.

In front of him stretched a line of barbed-wire fence and a gate, and a tall wooden stand with black fire-beaters stacked against it. He'd seen them before: the "In Case of Fire" notices and the beaters for bashing out flames. But next to them was something he'd never seen. A row of dead bird and animal bodies nailed up by their tails and wings. He stared, fascinated and appalled at the same time.

Rain began to patter on the leaves, on the grass, on the wooden board with the dead things hanging there, and on him.

He heard Dad behind him, singing as he squelched along the path. Dad stopped too.

"What is it?" Simon asked. "What's it for?"

"It's a gamekeeper's board," Dad said. "It's a warning."

"Why? Who for?"

"Well, the gamekeeper has to protect the pheasants—see, over there, behind the wire? And these are vermin. He's shot them because they are pests. Magpies and crows, and weasels. Or is it a stoat?"

Dad had laughed then. "Meanwhile, the gamekeeper is fattening up the pheasants so that rich bastards can shoot them!"

Simon puzzled over it all the way home. He couldn't get it. Did the other birds look at the dead ones and think, *Oh, better keep off*, or did they smell death, or what? What was the point of looking after the pheasants so someone else could shoot them? What did *rich bastards* mean?

None of it made any sense.

Simon wonders what Dad would say about him having an air rifle now. He sort of knows that he'd understand. He wishes he could remember the song Dad was singing, back there in the woods. There weren't any woods close to where they lived. They must have driven there from the old house. What was Nina doing? Why wasn't she there too?

He hears voices. Real ones, not just the radio. Someone is talking to Nina. He strains to hear what they're saying.

Now he recognizes Leah's voice. "I'll get her if you want, if he's still sleeping. Then you can go on gardening."

"Thanks, Leah. That's thoughtful of you. And Ellie will be pleased. Simon's so...so grumpy with her these days."

"Well I think she's cute."

Nina laughs. "You might not if you had to live with her. You haven't got any sisters or brothers, have you?"

There's silence. Simon imagines Leah shaking her head. He knows the way her hair will swish sideways, shiny in the sunlight.

"Was that your new boyfriend who was here?" Leah asks.

Simon's ears are on full alert now.

Nina laughs again.

He waits to hear what she'll say, but Leah speaks again.

"He's good looking, isn't he?"

"Yes," Nina says, and laughs again.

Simon frowns. Something tight squeezes in his chest. He chucks the magazine onto the floor. He feels for the slingshot still stuffed in his pocket, loads it with a scrunched-up ball of paper, and practices shooting. He uses one of Ellie's toys as a target, a small bear she's left lying around. He gets it each time. Straight between the ears. He gets back on the bed and shoots from there. He's pretty accurate; he aims and gets the center of the window frame, the lampshade, the pile of books on the desk. After a while it gets boring and he just lies on the bed, staring into space.

He remembers the art homework he still hasn't done. He gets out his sketchbook, starts to draw his knife, just because it's there in front of him. He shades in the blade, to show the way the light catches it. He draws every detail of the rings of metal round the handle. It looks like crap. It's his dad's knife. He's not giving that to Mr. bloody Davies.

He twists the paper up and chucks it at the door. Then he lies back on the bed.

He must have slept, because the next thing he knows, Ellie's bouncing excitedly on the end of his bed, and Leah is standing at the open bedroom door, a half-smile curling her mouth.

"Hi," she says. "We came to check you were OK. You've been sleeping for ages. Your mum's gone out. I'm looking after Ellie."

His headache suddenly comes back with a vengeance. His temples throb, both sides, in addition to the bump on the top of his skull. The light's too bright. He closes his eyes. *How long have they been there watching me? Go away. Get out of my room.*

"We'll leave you to get up," Leah says. "Come on, Ellie."

Simon listens to their voices. Ellie's showing Leah everything in her room, chattering all the time, and Leah sounds all bright and interested. It's a put-on, Simon can tell.

"Going to get the rest of the camping stuff," he grunts at them a short while later on his way out through the garden.

Ellie sticks her head out of the bramble den. "Can we come?"

Leah's watching him. She stretches out her long tanned legs. She's wearing a really short skirt. In one hand she's holding a pink plastic teacup.

Simon feels sweat prickling his back. "No," he tells Ellie. He doesn't look at Leah's face. He leaves them to get on with their stupid game in the bramble den.

They left the tarpaulin and two backpacks in a hollow at
the base of a stone hedge, a field boundary, just off the footpath. He's almost there when he hears voices. Laughter.
Instinctively he stops, takes cover at the edge of the wall,
waits to see who it is. *Why didn't I get Johnny to come with
me?* His hand goes to his pocket, but the slingshot isn't
there. Neither is his knife. *Stupid.*

He knows that sneering voice. His heart thuds against
his ribs. Surely not here, this far out from the town? But it
is. It's Rick Singleton and a friend, a big guy, older than
Rick, and it seems they've found the camping stuff and are
now kicking it around, having a laugh. He hears something
metal clanking against stone. Fury wells up inside, but fear
too, curls round Simon's belly. There are two of them.
They're bigger than him. But it's his stuff. His and Dan's
and Johnny's. He can't just let them get away with it. The
big guy has wrapped the tarpaulin over his head now, and
he's whooping and flapping about with his arms outstretched like a demented superhero. They think they are
such a laugh. Rick Singleton has set up a line of bottles on
a rock and is chucking stones. Simon hears the *crack* of
splintering glass. They've got their backs to him at the moment. He could creep away unnoticed, coward that he is.
But something keeps him rooted to the spot. The way they
kick the stuff around. He remembers the seagull with the
broken wing, Rick and his buddies in a circle around it. He
ran away that time, didn't he? What does that make him?

Blood pounds in his ears. Something rustles in the wall
close to his shoulder. A shrew or something, rushing to and

fro in the ivy and moss, hunting out insects. There's that smell of hot earth, roots. Two buzzards circle high above the cliff. He's rooted to the spot, paralyzed. His muscles ache. *What do I do?*

Someone else is walking across the field. Simon hears the footsteps. His head spins. Surely they'll have seen him, will drag him out, and it'll be his head against the rock; he can see it, the way he'll be crouched in a ball, his hands over his face, while each one takes a turn at kicking his skull in.

Flap flap. Like a sail, or a kite.

But it's not the tarpaulin any more. It's a coat, flapping in the wind that's blowing strong off the sea, over the cliff and on to the fields. Simon looks up.

Mad Ed! It's that crazy man, climbing over the next stile and flapping his way over the field towards Rick Singleton. Simon should have guessed he'd be somewhere around, spooking everyone out with his gun and his blank eyes. Nina wouldn't listen this morning when he tried to tell her.

Rick and his pal stop, look at each other, shuffle closer. One of them says something; Simon can't hear what. But he's not hanging around to see what happens next. Now he's unfrozen, he's running back across the field, over the stile, back to the lane. All that matters for now is to get back home. Alive.

Ellie and Leah are still sitting in the bramble den, playing houses.

Simon goes into the dark kitchen and stands there, heart still thumping, wondering what to do next.

It feels as if danger is closing in, pressing him in on all sides. Coming closer.

14

21 July

We're going to meet one evening this week, if Simon's allowed out after what happened, and we might go back to that swimming place. He says there's somewhere else he wants to show me, some old burial place he's found. We were sitting in the bramble den with Ellie, and she was making us pretend cups of tea, with dolly cups and a plastic teapot and rose-petal water. He's quite sweet with her, really. Most of the time. (Though Ellie found her bear in his room with holes in it!!!) He was in bad shape after he got back from the fields. But he joined in Ellie's game. Ahh!

When Nina came back we heard her talking on the phone to her new boyfriend. She was laughing all the time. I guess she's in love. She doesn't seem like a mother when she's like that. I said I'd babysit Ellie so she can go out with him next Wednesday. That's the day Si gets out of school. I can't believe school's been going on all this time. It seems like another world. The GCSE results will be out in less than one month. Not that I care.

Simon Piper.

He's funny and cute; give him another four years or so and

he'll be cool and hunky. He is an outdoors freak. I haven't a clue what he's talking about some of the time. He knows lots of facts about things. We have quite a laugh. He is much nicer than I expected.

Matt Davies.

Has the bluest eyes. Dark hair that curls over his collar. His blue linen collar!! Mature. Sensitive. With the most soooo kissable lips. When he left their house this morning he looked right at me. That's twice now. The time in the bookshop. And today.

Nina Piper. Nina Davies.

Leah Davies.

I can feel that something is changing. Something is going to happen to me soon.

Leah lets the pen doodle along the diary page. It loops and spirals. She draws a butterfly. She draws another. Then a flower with a big round middle and five petals, like Ellie might draw. She gives it two eyes, then a mouth. A happy face, with turned-up lips in a smile. She draws a whole row of flowers, and then a smaller butterfly above them, and dotted lines to show the path of its flight, dipping from flower to flower: a series of brief encounters.

She daydreams a while longer about Matt Davies.

Simon's mum is too old for him. She must be nearly forty, and she doesn't exactly make an effort. Her hair, for instance. She should get highlights or some color, to cover up the grey bits. Leah reaches over to her dressing table and picks up her brush. She pulls it through her hair, feeling it tug on her scalp, making it tingle. She turns so the sun shines onto her hair and reflects off it like gold. Imagines his hand rearranging it, turning her into a painting.

Perhaps she can get Simon to wangle an invitation to his studio. They could go up there together.

She shifts closer to the window. Simon's house looks dead, everyone out. What time is it?

She's determined not to think about what's happening downstairs in her own house.

It's the last class, Monday afternoon. Only two days now till they get out. Simon and Pike are on their way to English. Johnny and Dan are in the other group (advanced). He's glad he's got Pike. He's even worse than Simon at spelling and reading aloud.

"Oi! Simon! I've been wanting to see you. Come here, please." Mr. Davies's voice.

Damn! He'd hoped to sidle past the art rooms without Mr. Davies noticing.

Pike looks at him and laughs. "Expect he's got a message for your mum." He's heard all about what happened over the weekend from Johnny and Dan.

"Shut up!" Simon says, shoving him. Pike nearly squashes some innocent girl walking down the corridor.

Mr. Davies frowns at them both. "Your art homework?" he asks Simon. "You've missed two, now, as well as a double class."

Simon hangs his head. "Haven't got it," he mutters.

"You mean, not got it with you now, or not done it, period?"

"Not done it."

"Excuse us," Mr. Davies says to Pike. "We need a little chat, Mr. Piper and I. Where are you two off to now?"

Mr. *Piper*. That was his dad. A shiver goes down

Simon's spine. How dare he! He'd like to punch Mr. Davies right there and then. He can't stand that teachery way of talking.

"English," Pike says. "With Miss Wooding."

"OK, Simon. I'll be brief. Step in here a moment."

"I'll tell Wooding for you." Pike grins at Simon. "Good luck."

Simon watches him disappear along the corridor. Now he feels totally alone.

Mr. Davies isn't expecting a class; he's got drawings laid out all over the tables: big charcoal ones, and pen-and-ink sketches, and one bright, beautiful abstract oil painting, like a peacock among the black-and-white drawings.

"Good, isn't it? One of my A-level students."

Simon nods. His palms are sweating.

"So, Simon, what's happening? With the homework? It's not like you."

"Haven't done it."

"Why not?"

Simon shrugs. "Don't know."

"Did you try?"

"I drew something. Tore it up."

"Why?"

"It was crap."

"Real reason?"

"Don't know."

Silence.

"I'll be late for English," Simon mumbles.

Mr. Davies's voice sounds peculiar, as if he's swallowed something and it's stuck in his throat. "Don't throw it all away, Simon. Not now. Just as some sort of petty

133

protest . . ."

Simon can't speak. Something's welling up inside him: a huge fury, waiting to spill out in a torrent of filthy words. But he doesn't say anything.

Mr. Davies coughs, then he speaks more slowly and quietly, as if he's deliberately calming himself down. "Your artwork has been fantastic. What I've seen since May. You have a rare talent. So just do one homework. For tomorrow. OK? Fresh start next term, for the new GCSE course."

"Can't."

"What do you mean, can't?"

"I can't draw. Not at the moment."

"Can't, or won't? This isn't something to do with . . . with your mother and me, by any remote chance?"

Simon's gone hot all over and then suddenly freezing.

Mr. Davies moves away towards the window. Simon looks up. Mr. Davies has his back to Simon and is staring at the sky. There's a gull high up. Mr. Davies has both his hands in his pockets.

"OK," he says slowly, turning round to face Simon. "I guess we all have blocks from time to time. Creative people. Artists. Let's leave it, this time. We can make a fresh start next term. I'm sorry it's hard for you right now. It'll get better."

He's backed down completely! Simon can hardly believe it.

Mr. Davies starts picking up drawings off the table and examining them. "You could do stuff as good as this. Better, even."

"Can I go now?" Simon asks. He feels slightly sick.

Mr. Davies sighs heavily. "Yes. Don't forget, Simon.

You're welcome at the studio, any time. Come with Nina over vacation."

Simon's head is throbbing. He walks out of the art room without speaking. He doesn't know what to think.

He's fifteen minutes late for English, but Miss Wooding doesn't mind. She's showing them an old black-and-white film of *To Kill a Mockingbird*. It'll be one of their required-reading texts next term. He doesn't really take any of it in.

Pike comes down to town with him after school. They take the bus all the way to the bus station, and then they walk along the seafront and down along the harbor wall. Pike's dad is a fisherman, though not at this harbor. He works on a trawler at Newlyn. Pike doesn't think there'll be any fishing fleet left by the time he's ready to work.

"That's only two years," Simon says. "Unless you go to college."

"What for?" Pike says. He gets a crabbing line out of his pocket, sticks a bit of old sandwich on the hook and dangles it down over the harbor wall into the deep green water. "We need some proper bait really," he says. "Bacon, or sand eels."

Simon leans back against the warm stones of the harbor wall. His head still aches, but it's kind of comforting being with Pike.

There's a figure of a man shambling along the pier end of the harbor. He seems familiar. Simon watches him for a while. He looks odd. He's wearing a long heavy coat, even though it's so sunny. Of course. It's him again. "There's that crazy guy," he says to Pike. "Who nearly shot me and Dan and John at the weekend." He doesn't tell him about what happened later with Rick Singleton. He hasn't told anyone about that, or about what he found when he finally went back in the evening to see if he could retrieve his stuff; how he found it all neatly packed up, back in the bag, and how three large shells had been placed on the folded tarp. Oyster shells. He shivers, remembering.

Pike laughs. "He's all right," he says. "He just likes to keep an eye on things, that's what my dad reckons."

Simon pulls a face. "But he's still weird. Look at him. In that old coat. What's he carrying, anyway?"

They both watch the man as he comes closer. Now they can see what it is in his arms.

"It's a bloody huge seagull," Pike says. "A young one."

"What's he doing? Told you he was weird!"

The bird is struggling to get free, flapping its speckledy wings and twisting its neck. Close up now, Simon can see something's wrong with its beak. The man stops every so often and seems to put his hand right inside. The bird flails and flaps and squirms, but it can't squawk.

"It's got something stuck," Pike says. "Fishing hook, probably. They swallow them sometimes. Trying to get the fish. Stupid things."

They watch. The man's managed to get the hook out. The bird lets out a huge croak and wriggles its neck, and then Mad Ed lets it go, throws it up into the air, and the bird flaps and finds its own strength and soars away.

"What's the point?" Pike asks. "There are too many gulls already."

Rick Singleton comes into Simon's mind again: him and his friends, circling that young gull. He wonders whether they broke the wing in the first place, and what they did to the bird after he'd gone.

"Pity you can't eat them," Simon says. "What do you reckon they'd taste like?"

"Rotten fish. Garbage. Vomit."

Mad Ed has shambled off again. They watch him go farther along the wall and sit down on a bench.

"I wonder what he's doing in town," Pike says. "He stays up on the cliffs, usually. Or at the farm."

"He gives me the creeps," Simon says. "He's watching us, you know."

"That's what people always say. But what's wrong with it? We're watching him, aren't we?"

Pike's got no imagination, Simon thinks. *He always thinks the best of everyone.* Simon wonders whether to tell him what happened up at the burial mound, and about the slingshot. But when he thinks how to say it, it doesn't sound like anything worth telling Pike. Pike would just find some perfectly logical explanation.

"We're not going to get any crabs," Pike says. "They're not that stupid. They know we've only got bread on the hook."

"We should come back," Simon says. "Bring proper bait. Or we could fish off the rocks. And make a fire, cook fish and crab and stuff. Let's do it on Wednesday. For the last day of school. They'll let us out early, won't they?"

Pike nods. He pulls up the crabbing line.

Mad Ed's still watching them as they make their way back along the harbor, but Simon doesn't mention it again.

On the way up the hill to his house he starts thinking about Leah. He's supposed to be meeting her tomorrow. He can't tell Pike about that, either.

Tuesday evening. Leah watches from her bedroom window. She's arranged to meet Simon at eight. She's been ready for ages. He appears at his gate at exactly five past. She goes down to meet him.

"Ready?" She smiles at him.

He nods.

"What did you tell Nina?"

"Said I was going for a walk. To see the burial mound. She liked that. It's *history*. I said I might do some drawings. So it's *art* too."

She can see a small sketchpad stuffed into his pocket.

"You didn't mention me, then?"

He doesn't answer.

"She's going to borrow some more books about stone burial chambers for me. I've been reading about the history of this place—ancient history, you know?"

Not really. But Leah makes a mental note to try and take an interest.

"Why do you want to show me, anyway?" she asks Simon.

"I want to see if anything . . . happens. Like before."

What's he going on about? She remembers him saying something about hitting his head; she wasn't really paying attention. He looks a bit weird this evening. Or maybe it's just the light, all red and gold over him as they walk down the lane to the path. He walks slightly ahead of her as usual. He walks too fast. Every so often she has to jog to catch him up. She notices the hairs on his legs where he's rolled up his blue trousers, his leather walking boots. Matt Davies might have looked a bit like this about sixteen years ago. Sixteen years! She'd have been just a baby!

She clambers over the stile after Simon, into the tunnel of trees that marks the beginning of the footpath.

He turns and waits for her to catch up. "This is called the Coffin Path," he says.

She gives an obliging shiver. "Creepy," she says.

"They used to take the coffins this way from the farms when people died. To the church. I've been reading about it."

Right. Whatever. Why's he telling her this?

"But the burial chamber is much older than that," he goes on. "Five thousand years. Neolithic."

"Is it far?" She's wearing flip-flops. Her feet ache.

"No. Not really."

They come out of the trees, over another stile, into a field. She shivers for real. Bare arms, midriff—should have brought a jacket.

"It's always windy here," Simon says. "Come on. You'll warm up if we walk faster."

Her flip-flops click against her heels as she shuffles over the rough grass track. After a while she takes them off and walks barefoot. The grass feels surprisingly warm.

The sun's dropped low now, behind the hill. The sky's a fantastic turquoise color, like silk. Leah stumbles, grabs Simon's arm. "Whoops!" She hangs on.

He has to match his pace to hers, though all the time it feels as if he's chafing to get away and go faster.

"Why don't you wear proper shoes?" Simon asks, as she stops again to pick a small stone from her heel.

She shrugs. "How far now?"

"Another two fields, I think."

At the stile she sits for a moment on the top stone. It's

broad enough, almost like a seat. She closes her eyes. "Tired," she says to Simon, like a small child on a too-long walk.

"That's where they would have rested the coffin," Simon says. "Where you are."

She shivers again. What did he have to say that for? He's winding her up and it's beginning to get to her, all this stuff about coffins and dead people. Even if it was a long time ago.

She climbs down the other side. "So, what happened the other night?" Leah looks into his face and watches the flush spread over his cheeks.

"I'm—I'm not sure, exactly; I came over all funny when I went in the stone chamber and, next thing, I was lying on the ground outside with a sore head."

Leah laughs. "*How* much did you say you'd had to drink?"

But her laugh hangs uneasily in the air. She wishes it wasn't getting dark. This doesn't seem such a good idea now.

"You can see it now, there." Simon points to a dark shape across the field. It's not what she expected; it's bigger, for one thing. They get closer. Two huge stones guard the entrance. The roof is grassed over. Her flesh begins to tingle. She grabs Simon's arm again.

"What was it for?"

"A place to put the dead, I suppose. Or maybe just their bones. Inside, there are lots of separate chambers, like little rooms. It goes in a long way and it sort of slopes back into the ground. It feels as if you're going down deep."

She wishes she hadn't said she'd come.

"So, are you coming?" Simon asks. "Or would you rather stay and guard the entrance?"

"I'm not staying out here by myself," Leah says. She peers into the mouth of the chamber. *It's so dark!* "Get your flashlight."

Simon pulls out the sketchpad and then flashlight torch. He leaves the pad on the grass. He takes his slingshot from his other pocket and keeps it in his hand as they go in. He gives her the flashlight.

The beam of light thins into the darkness. It hardly makes any difference, just a small pinprick immediately in front of the flashlight. She's shaking.

"You could wait here," Simon says, "and I'll go farther in and see what happens this time."

"No way."

"Come on, then."

She takes his arm again and slides her hand down until it's lightly touching his. She feels his hand go taut, and then relax. His fingers curl round hers.

She's never been anywhere so dark. The flashlight beam makes one tiny pool on the stone ceiling when you shine it up, but directed ahead of them, the light just bounces back. Their voices too, are swallowed up by the darkness.

She feels the dry earth under her feet. To begin with it feels cold, and then something seems to happen. Her fear drains away. Her body starts tingling all over and a warm feeling flows up through her feet, up her legs, her thighs, her belly. She can feel the pulse of Simon's heart through her fingertips. She has a sudden yearning to bury her head into his chest, though she doesn't.

Her head begins to spin.

"Can you feel it?" she whispers, and tugs him closer. He's so close now she can smell his faint, musky male smell. He turns, and she senses rather than sees that his face is right next to hers, almost touching, but not quite.

"What?"

"How warm it is, and sort of . . . alive. The stone."

His breath is warm on her cheek.

"It feels amazing," she says. "It's magic or something. What is it?"

"I don't know. There's no sound, though. Our voices don't echo, like you'd expect. The sound is sucked away. I can hardly hear you, even though you're so close."

She can hear a tremble in his voice. "You're shaking," she says. "Are you all right?" Her voice is unexpectedly tender. What's happening to her?

"Yes—no—you—"

She lets her lips brush against his face. "It's OK," she whispers. "Us. Here."

His lips touch hers. She puts her arms right around him, presses his spine, feels his body go tight. Then the tingling in her own body takes over and she starts to feel dizzy.

He pulls away from her. "Got to get out!" He stumbles out of the stone chamber, and she follows, grabbing onto his T-shirt for dear life, as if she will drown alone in the darkness. Then they both lean against the entrance stones, shocked at the sudden explosion of all their senses as they come out into the cool air, feel the wind and the rough grass. The whole sky seems to open up above them, studded with a million trillion stars.

They are both still shaking.

Leah comes to. She begins to giggle. "Wow!" she says. "That was amazing! What was it in there? Like a force field, or trapped energy or something. All warm and alive. Like being inside something living." She laughs again. "Like being back in the womb!"

He can't look at her, he's so shy. But in the deep, secret darkness, he kissed her. He did! And the truly amazing thing is, she liked it.

He's moved away from her now, as if nothing happened. He's young, he's never kissed anyone before. She can be patient.

"That time before," she says softly. "You must have felt it too, whatever it is in there, and needed air, and hit your head on the stone as you came out. Something like that."

She watches him pick up the damp sketchpad from the grass. A snail has left a silvery trail over the cover.

"Got to get back," he says. "I mustn't be late."

"Sketching in the dark!" Leah giggles. "Never mind. Nina's easy on you, isn't she? Compared to—to most parents."

She chatters on as they walk back across the fields. The grass has cooled right down now. Her feet are freezing. Simon barely answers, but she doesn't mind. She can't wait till she gets back home and can write this all up in her diary. She knows it's important in some way that isn't clear to her yet. It links up with something bigger. Part of what's meant to be.

She wonders what Simon's thinking about as they walk. Her? The stone place? Telling his friends?

She knows for sure that he won't want anyone seeing them coming up the lane together. She tells him to go on ahead, and she waits until his door has clicked shut before she walks the last fifty yards to her own front door. It's locked. She has to tiptoe around to the back, ducking under the lit window at the side, and creep in the back way through the kitchen, up the stairs to her room. Voices mur-mur from the sitting room.

She washes her face and then her feet, balancing one foot at a time on the basin. She stares at herself in the mir-ror, purses her lips up in a kiss. She slips into bed without turning on the light, doesn't write in her diary after all. Too tired. It's hot and stuffy in her room; she crawls out of bed and flings the window wide open. There's the sweet smell of some wild flower wafting up from the yard. The creamy petals glow in the dark.

She lies on her back under a thin sheet, keeping com-pletely still, practicing being dead. She dreams in the night that her legs have turned to stone.

15

Each day's hotter than the last. It hasn't rained since that Saturday when Simon took her to the swimming cove down the cliff. There's nothing to do all day except keep out of the way. She's bored with sunbathing all by herself.

When she went over to babysit on Wednesday, Nina had chatted to her while she got ready to meet Matt.

"Why don't you get yourself a job? It doesn't matter what, really. Just to earn some money and keep you busy while you work out what to do next. Don't your parents mind you hanging around all day?"

Leah didn't tell Nina that they had other things to worry about right now.

"My childminder, Rita, might be able to help?" Nina offered. "You could get more babysitting through her probably. You're good with Ellie. What about a childcare course in September? At the college."

Leah just shrugged. "I've had enough of learning things."

Nina had looked sad when she said that.

Simon had gotten back about ten. He hadn't wanted her to stay. "Mum left your money in the kitchen," he said.

"You can go now I'm back."

"Do you want a coffee or something? I'll make you one if you like."

"No. I'm tired. I'm going to bed."

And that had been that. It was as if he'd forgotten all about their walk, the kiss. He didn't even look at her, not really. He smelt of wood smoke and booze. She supposed he'd been out with those kids from school. End of the year.

She heard Nina's car about eleven. Early. Perhaps they'd had an argument. Maybe he's realized she's not right for him after all. Too old and sensible. And who'd want to take on two children like that? When they could have someone young and exciting and free?

It's too hot in the yard now. Leah swings her legs round off the patio chair and goes into the kitchen to get a glass of water. She thinks about that cove again, where she swam with Simon. Why not? There must be a quicker way to get there, if she cuts across the fields. If she finds that path again, Simon's Coffin Path. It won't be spooky in the day-time.

She walks quietly upstairs to get a towel, grabs an apple from the bowl in the kitchen on her way out. No one sees her go.

She's hotter than ever by the time she finds the right place, sweat trickling down her back. There's the brief, terrifying moment when she has to get the rope and swing herself over the edge, lower herself hand over hand, but she does it. She almost wishes there was someone to see, someone to admire her. But of course there's no one around for miles.

It's hot even on the rocks today, hardly a breath of

wind. She peers down to the swimming cove. It looks different. The tide is high, she supposes. You can't see the sandy bottom like she could last time they were here. How will she get back out? Simon had to help her last time.

Leah steps back from the edge. She might as well make the most of the sun. She peels off her sticky T-shirt, her bra, her skirt and pants. She can get her all-over suntan at last. She dangles her legs down over the side of the rocks so her feet trail in the sea; it cools her down just enough. Then she finds a place to lie out flat on her towel.

No one can see her. No one knows she's here. She's free as the birds circling overhead, mewing in the high blue sky. She loses track of time. Dozes. Every so often she strokes her body with another layer of tanning lotion, for a perfect golden tan.

Suddenly, a sharp sound like gunshot rips out, echoes and reverberates off the cliff. Leah sits up, grabs her T-shirt, scans the cliff face. What was it? She can see a small trickle of chalky rock crumbling down the top of the rough track. Is someone there? She waits, holding her clothes like a shield, but nothing more happens. The birds are wheeling overhead again, unperturbed.

It must have been from farther away. Sound travels long distances over the fields.

She's unbearably hot. The sea washes against the rocks, soothing and inviting. She knows how cold it will be, but she can't resist. She works out the easiest place for getting in and out. There are only tiny waves: the cove's sheltered from the wind. She can swim well enough. She steps down on to the lower platform of rock, slides herself over the edge. She gasps, then dips right in, lets go of the rock and starts to swim. With the sun full on her face, it's just about bearable. To begin with, she stays close to the rocks. She turns onto her back. Paddling with her arms to keep herself still she scans the cliff, checking that no one is watching her. She'll stay in for the count of fifty, and then she'll get out and warm up again.

16

Simon can't concentrate on the *Ancient Stones* book because every time he looks at the pages on Neolithic burial chambers, he sees Leah's face close up. Not that he could see it, there in the dark. And he feels peculiar, because of what happened. What he did, without planning it or meaning anything. It was because it was so hot in there and she was so close. Her mouth tasted like . . . like nothing at all he can think of. There was a sensation, like falling, and a smell, something remembered from a long time ago. It's just out of his reach. So now it seems it does mean something after all. That kiss.

His head's all muddled up. He needs to run, or get on his bike, or swim, or shoot something.

It's the holidays, but everyone's away now. Pike, Johnny, Dan . . . Nina wanted him to sign up for surfing lessons. Surfing is what everyone does around here. She'd rather he learned safely. But he won't know anyone there. Can't face it. Today she's taken Ellie down to the beach. He might join them later. But before that, he's going to check out a web site for air rifles. He doesn't have a credit card, though, so he can't order it off the Net. He'll have to find another way.

You're supposed to be eighteen. Pike or Johnny's dad would get him one if he asked, but he can't wait that long. He could work on Mum, but the time's not right.

He switches the computer on. It calms him down, scrolling through the different types of gun. Something inside him shifts back to normal. The one he wants is called a Supersport.

He plays a quick game of "Monkey Lander" and then he watches the end of a film he recorded the other night off TV. It takes his mind off things, watching a load of gangsters getting shot, and a car chase, but he ends up feeling even more wired up. He'll get his bike out.

He takes the road he walked down that day after school; it's uphill almost all the way, but he makes himself do it without stopping, till he's sweating and red-faced and his heart's pounding. The muscles in his legs feel tight. It's good to push yourself. That's how you get stronger. Once he's at the high point of the road the view is fantastic, right across the patchwork of fields and stone hedges to the sea. There's hardly any wind. He peels off the main road down a small track in the direction of the sea. It passes through a small cluster of stone buildings: a house, a barn. A studio. He got there by instinct, he'll think later. He hadn't meant to, not consciously.

He knows who the man will be, weeding a row of beans in the walled garden, even before the man raises his head and stands up.

"Simon! How nice!"

So he has to stop, doesn't he?

"Hi." His voice comes out in a sort of growl.

"You look hot! Come and have a drink."

Simon dismounts, leans the bike against the wall, finds himself trailing after Matt Davies into the house. For a second he can't see a thing. His eyes adjust to the green light of a small kitchen.

Matt takes a bottle of beer out of the fridge. "Want one? Or Coke?"

"Just water. Thanks."

Matt pulls a face. "Suit yourself." He runs the kitchen tap and then fills a glass for Simon. He gets ice from the freezer. The ice chinks against the glass. It's like being in a film. Sound effects. The bottle being opened, a chair scraping over a wooden floor. Simon looks around the room. There are huge framed charcoal drawings on three walls. Abstract landscapes or something.

Matt watches him. "What do you think? he asks. "Like them?"

Simon blushes. "They're good," he says. "Did you do them?"

"I did. They're part of a series. For an exhibition a few years back. Want to see some other stuff? Since you're here?"

Simon nods. "I was just out biking. I didn't know your house was here." He doesn't want Matt Davies to think he came on purpose, even if he has been invited, more than once, to see the studio.

Matt grins. "Whatever. But I'm glad you came. And since you're here, you might as well take a look. Come and see my new work in the studio. More water?"

He refills their glasses. "Thirsty weather," he says to Simon. "Especially when you're working. Or biking."

Simon follows him across the garden to the studio attached to the barn. It's got a glass roof and is full of light and white stone dust. A set of stone carving tools are laid out along the bench just inside the door. There's a sketchbook of rough pencil drawings propped up on the bench against the wall. A huge chunk of pale stone sits on a cloth on the floor. It doesn't look like anything yet.

Simon wrinkles up his nose at the smell. He likes it; an earthy, chalky smell. Stone. Paint. Turpentine. Further in, there are more drawings and slabs of stone, and some big paintings. They seem to be a mixture of landscapes and life drawings. Naked women, back views. Or bits of the body. He doesn't look too closely. Matt moves back and stands in front of some of the pictures, half hiding them. It's as if he's suddenly seeing the studio through Simon's eyes and realizing what is there.

Matt coughs slightly. "They're life studies, for the stone sculpture," he explains, awkwardly. "It's hot in here. Let's go back to the garden."

What's the matter with him? Why's he so nervous, suddenly?

There's a drawing of a woman turned to one side. He sees it, and blood rushes to his head. He knows her instantly. How could he not? It's his own mother.

He goes dizzy. He stumbles towards the door. "Too hot," he manages to mumble. He can see the handlebars of his bike along the edge of the wall; all he has to do is get there without passing out.

Matt Davies reaches out a hand. "Simon," he says, "I didn't think. Sorry. It's just what artists do, life drawing. It doesn't mean anything."

But it should, shouldn't it? Simon thinks as he hurtles

down the track away from the house. *When someone takes their clothes off for you like that. Shouldn't it?*

What else has she done to be helpful?

Urgh! He feels sweaty and disgusting, thinking about them. His mother and Mr. Davies. The bike skids over stones and gravel as the track peters out into grass. Stone hedges on either side press in; the air's thick with the rank smell of hot grass roots, nettles, rosebay willowherb.

His mother must have been sitting up there in his studio, while Matt Davies looked and drew and shaded and measured and turned her into art. He's making a sculpture of her body. It'll be in an exhibition, for the whole world to see. "Your mum, screwing a teacher!" *Johnny's words. Everyone will know.*

All these years it has been him and Ellie and Mum. There hasn't been anyone else, and he's never even thought about it. Why would there be anyone? She loved Dad and missed him like crazy at first, and then gradually she just got on with things, that's what she told Simon, making a life for them, and her. Like they all have. It faded, the thought of Dad, but it was still there all the time in the background. Safely there, like something solid you knew was still behind you. Would always be.

He thinks of the photograph Mum keeps on her bedside table. A young-looking Dad, with dark hair and blue eyes. What would he say about what Mum is doing? But that's a stupid way to think, isn't it? Dad can't say anything. Hasn't for years. Never will again. Doesn't know anything about Mum, or Ellie, or him, what their lives are now. He's dead. Dust and ashes. Gone.

The sun has bleached all the color from the sky. The whole cliff shimmers with heat. Simon dismounts the bike now the path has become so narrow and rocky, and pushes along. His muscles ache. It's like pushing through molasses. No, not molasses. Through something heavy and unyielding. Molten lead. Or water, against the current. Swimming against the riptide. You don't stand a chance.

Sweat's dripping into his eyes. He follows the path blindly, stumbling over jutting rocks, snagging his calves on brambles and gorse. Doesn't know where he's going, or why. Doesn't know anything any more.

He's so hot he's forced to stop. He pulls his T-shirt over his head, wipes his face with it and shoves it on the back of the bike. He goes and sits as close as he can to the edge of the cliff. He hasn't been on this stretch of the coast before. It's wild and steep. He can see something jutting out just below: stone overgrown with grass. Another burial mound? But when he gets closer he sees it's concrete, not stone. An old war bunker. He edges around, looking for a way in. There's a locked metal door covered in graffiti, and the stink of piss. He peers through the gun slits at the side, but all he can see is dust and darkness. There are bunkers like this all along the coast. Men would have been stationed here, training their binoculars over the stretch of Atlantic searching for submarines. He tries to imagine what it would have been like, watching and waiting for something that might or might not be there. But it's too hot. Simon kicks the door hard before he scrambles back up the cliff to the path.

Far, far below, something bobs up and down in the sea near an outcrop of black rocks. A seal. From here it looks a bit like a human head. That's probably the origin of those stories people tell about mermaids. Ellie's favorite story at the moment is about a woman who turns into a seal. A selkie. Ellie and Nina will be wondering whether he's going to turn up on the beach. Perhaps he will. There's something comforting about the thought of lying out on the sand next to his mum or digging channels from rock pools with Ellie. Just like it was before . . .

Before what? He's not even sure how to think of it. Before everything started to change: Mum, him.

Leah's face looms into his consciousness again. Her silky hair brushing against his arm. Her soft mouth. But the thought makes him cringe at the same time. Pleasure and disgust in equal measure.

He fires an imaginary air gun at the seal's head. It's closer now, looking up at him with its whiskery face. They went to a seal sanctuary once, him and Mum. He was only little. There was a small white pup in the hospital area being fed milk every four hours. Mum could hardly tear herself away. Simon wanted to watch the two big seals by the outside pool who were doing peculiar and fascinating things to each other. He didn't know what, at the time. Seals having sex. All that noise and blubber and wetness.

Simon picks up the bike from where he abandoned it and pushes it slowly along the path for another mile. He starts to recognize landmarks. He's back on home ground.

Just when he's starting to relax, a shot rips out. It's that crazy guy again. Why's he shooting rabbits in the middle of the day? Because he's nuts, that's why. Any sane person's lying in the shade or on a beach somewhere. Or on vacation. Simon doesn't feel like meeting Mad Ed again right now. He's unarmed, he's got the bike, it's too hot. Three good enough reasons. He waits, listens, then wheels along a bit further. He locks the bike to a stumpy hawthorn tree and peers over the cliff edge to see if he can get down to the rocks nearer the sea. That's when he sees Leah.

At first he thinks it's another seal bobbing around. But it's a seal with long hair and golden arms. What does she think she's doing? How stupid can you get? It's not even an ordinary low tide, let alone a spring low tide, which is the only time it's really safe to swim from the cove. Perhaps he should have made a bigger thing of it. He never thought she'd walk out here by herself, and certainly not climb down the cliff and get in the sea. *She's bonkers too*, he thinks. But as he watches her splashy backstroke across the little cove, he starts thinking how delicious it looks. Cool, sparkling sea. It's what he needs more than anything at this precise moment. He starts running along the cliff towards the fence where the rope's tied.

She must have seen him. He hears her cry out, her voice a thin sound mixed with all the others: seagulls, waves, the throb of an unseen fishing boat. He can't hear the actual words, and he doesn't dare look down mid-rappel.

By the time he's gotten right down to the water, she's blue-lipped and shivering. Close up, he sees her scratched and bleeding hands from where she's tried to cling on to the ledge. Her teeth are chattering so much he can't make out what she's saying. He leans over, grabs her hand.

"Are you OK? It's dangerous here—the tide—grab on."

She's exhausted, has hardly any strength. He heaves her arm and body, winces as her skin tears on the rough rock. He tries to look away as she scrabbles up, but he can't help seeing everything. Not a mermaid, then. Not a seal.

He's aware of her cowering behind her dry clothes, clutching them like Ellie might hold a teddy. She's shaking violently.

She doesn't look anything like the Leah he's known so far. She struggles back into her clothes and sits hunched against the cliff, cowed and beaten and utterly vulnerable. "I couldn't get out," she stammers over and over. "The sea was dragging me away from the rock." She starts to cry. "What if you hadn't come?"

"You shouldn't have swum," he tells her. "It's dangerous, unless it's a spring tide. You know, an extra low tide. At full moon. Like when we were here before. There are currents. A riptide."

"Why didn't you explain that before?"

"I didn't think you'd come back. I should have said. I'm sorry."

Stop crying. Shut up, he'd like to say. *Nothing happened. You're all right.*

He looks down at his feet. His hands feel too big. He's sweating like a pig. All he wanted was to cool down, and now look.

The heat presses down. A small brown lizard flicks its tongue as it suns itself on a rock. Simon watches it. He could catch it in one hand if he were quick. You have to be careful, otherwise the tail drops off.

A sudden shift and trickle of soil and gravel sliding down the cliff sends the lizard darting under a stone. Simon and Leah both stare up at the cliff face. There's someone there. They can see a shadow. Simon feels Leah's hand on his arm. She's shaking.

17

"**It happened before,**" Leah whispers.

"What?"

"Stones falling down the cliff. The sound of a gun. It's that creepy guy, I bet." She shudders. "Watching me. Weirdo pervert." She starts to giggle.

It's no laughing matter. Mad Ed, with a gun. Again. There's no place to hide. It would be like picking off crows. Not that Simon *seriously* believes Mad Ed will try to kill them. Does he?

"Have you met him?" Simon asks Leah.

"Not really. But I've seen him, heard about him. Everyone's heard about him around here. He used to hang around the town, ages back. He got into trouble with the police for watching people—families, children—on the beach or something. People complained."

"Sshh. Listen."

There's another trickle of soil from the cliff. The buzzards wheeling over the moor are circling higher. The lizard flicks its tongue under the rock.

"I'm going up. To see."

"Be careful," Leah says. She lets go of his arm.

It's a kind of test he sets himself, to see if he can do things that scare him.

Both his slingshot and his knife are still in his bag, strapped to the bike. Stupid, to leave them there. He imagines he's being filmed as he scrambles up the cliff. Gracefully he swings up over the top, gun ready for enemy fire.

Nothing there. A breeze ruffles the dried grass and the pale pink cushions of sea thrift that grow along the edge. When he looks down to wave at Leah he feels dizzy. He's just about to yell down that there's no one there when he notices a small ring of stones. Not a circle, he realizes as he gets closer: a shape like a heart. Each stone is the perfect size for the slingshot, like the ones he found before on the stile that night. His heart begins to thud. What does it mean? Is it a message? A warning?

Simon scatters the heart with his foot. He can't see anyone, but this cliff dips and curves so much anyone could have walked out of sight in the time it took him to climb up the cliff. It's seriously spooky. The slingshot stones on the stile, now these. And something else is nagging at the back of his mind. Those oyster shells left on the neat pile of camping stuff. Was that him too?

Now Leah's huffing up the cliff after him. He won't tell her about the stones. She climbs over the fence and he glimpses the smooth golden skin of her stomach and something inside him flips and squirms all over again. *Leah, naked in the sea. Him pulling her out.*

What would Dan or Johnny or Pike think, seeing him like this? They never talk about girls, the four of them. They pretend they don't exist most of the time, the same way the girls in their grade just ignore them. It's not the same with all the ninth-grade boys, it's just that they are in a different league altogether. Dan, Pike, John, and him, they're just not into clothes, or music, or being cool. Or going out with girls.

"I'm going back the quick way," Leah says. "The way you didn't tell me about. Like you didn't tell me about the tides. Coming?"

"I'm m-meeting Mum and Ellie down the town beach," Simon stammers. "I've got my bike."

"See you, then."

"You'll be all right? With that man moping around?"

Leah gives him a scornful look. "Why? You offering to defend me?"

He feels himself blush. It's a relief to watch her flounce off, flip-flops clacking.

The handlebars on the bike have heated up in the sun. The bike smells of hot metal, rubber, leather. He checks that the knife and slingshot are still in the bag, then re-trieves them and puts them in his pocket instead. That man might be waiting farther up.

The coast path's too bumpy and uneven to ride and he ends up pushing the bike most of the way. At last he gets to the blacktop path and scoots down the hill to the town beach.

It's thick with people. How's he ever going to find Mum and Ellie? Maybe they've gone home by now. At last he spots them, down at the sea's edge, paddling in the shallow waves. He keeps wheeling over people's mats and towels by mistake as he weaves his way across the sand between all the little family groups. People *tut* at him as if he's doing it on purpose.

"Simon!" Ellie runs across the wet sand waving a fishing net at him. "We're catching little fishes. Look! They're all silvery."

"Sand eels," he tells her. "They make terrific bait."

But Ellie is peering intently into her bucket. He watches her tip them back out into the sea. Their silver bodies flash in the sunlight as they swim free.

"My head aches," Simon says.

"Have a rest under the umbrella," Nina says. "You look exhausted. Too much biking in this heat. Drink some water too. There's a bottle in the bag."

He dozes in the shade, lets their voices wash over him and the sound of the waves lull him, and for a little while he can forget everything. He opens his eyes. Ellie in her little swimsuit is pouring wet sand through her fingers to make a fairy castle. Nina lolls on her towel, reading. There are bodies everywhere, soaking up the sunshine. Female bodies, mostly. The boys are all running and clambering on rocks and rushing in and out of the sea and yelling and digging water channels; skinny bodies that are all bone and sinew and muscle, busy doing things. He sees more clearly than ever the differences, male and female. It's not just their bodies, it's the way they are. The way they move and speak and everything.

"Why don't you swim?" Nina asks.

"I haven't got my swimming stuff."

"Just go in your shorts."

"I'm going home," he grunts at her. He hates the beach suddenly and ferociously.

"Pleeeease stay," Ellie wheedles. "Make me one of those

huge castles you do with the moat and everything. And a water channel. Please please please!"

Nina doesn't say anything, but he can feel the pressure on him to stay and play with his sister like a hand pressing down on his head. It's too strong; he relents. He takes Ellie's spade and marks out the rough circle for a castle down near the water so they can watch the incoming tide invade it. The sand squidges between his toes, cools his hot feet. He immerses himself in the simple, familiar task of building a sandcastle and lets Ellie's chatter shut out everything else. She's so happy to have him play with her, she dances round him, getting under his feet.

"Find some shells," he instructs her, "for the top."

"Smile for the camera," Nina says. They pose for her next to the finished castle, grinning. For some strange reason she has tears in her eyes.

The tide creeps up the beach. It's the best time, when the waves first start to lick and curl round the outer defenses of the castle, and they can still mend the small breaches with wet sand and pebbles, ready for the next onslaught. You know what will happen: it's unstoppable, but that doesn't stop you pitting yourself against it, damming and shoring up in a race against the tide. When the final assault comes, and the inner keep is swamped and dissolved back to sand, it doesn't feel like a defeat at all. Simon can't help laughing and whooping at the delight of it, like the little boy he used to be, playing unselfconsciously on the sand.

"Time to pack up," Nina says.

"Just a little bit longer," Ellie pleads.

There are fewer people on the beach now. It's the best

time to swim, with the sea coming in over warmed sand. Simon strips off quickly down to his boxers and runs and shallow dives into the waves that are curling up the beach. Once he's through the breaking point of the waves, he turns and lies on his back, floating. It's unbelievably delicious to be wet and cool after such a day.

"You come in too," he calls to Nina. "It's really warm."

She laughs. "Yeah, I believe you!" But she starts to paddle out, and then a breaking wave catches her full on and drenches her. She squeals.

"You might as well now!" Simon shouts.

Ellie wails from the beach, left behind. Nina swims out to join Simon in the deep turquoise water. They haven't done this for years. He splashes her and she yelps and splashes back and as the waves get bigger, they start to bodysurf on them, back toward the shore.

"What about me?" Ellie's voice pipes out over the water.

"Too dangerous for you," Nina splutters. "You have to be able to swim properly first, Ellie. But I'm coming out in a minute, I'm freezing!"

When she's back on the beach drying herself, Simon turns back and swims, crawl, right out beyond the breaking waves, letting each roller lift and bounce his body as he crosses them.

"Not too far out!" Her voice is faint, he can hardly hear her.

He swims as far as he dares out into the bay. He thinks of all the sea beneath him, down and down. Not far beyond him is the thin line of white water which marks the riptide. He floats a moment, watching the way the water boils and chafes on the current, and then he turns and swims back towards his mother and sister on the beach.

They've already packed everything away. Nina holds out a towel. "That was too far. Don't, for my sake."

He grins, shivering, exhilarated.

"We'll start walking. You can catch up on the bike, yes?"

"Can't I go on the bike? I'm tired," Ellie whines.

"I'm not pushing you all the way up that hill," Simon says.

"We'll get you an ice cream, Ellie. You'll be all right."

In the end they all three have an ice cream. Simon leans the bike against the sea wall to eat his while Nina and Ellie plod on back through the town.

From where he's sitting, he can see into the amusement arcade, and a gang of boys firing in the shooting range. He recognizes Rick Singleton. The eel in his stomach flips again. But Rick isn't with his friends this time. He has one arm round a girl with long dark hair and the shortest shorts. He doesn't notice Simon.

Simon bikes the long way home. The others are there already. Leah is sitting at the kitchen table.

18

She looks as if she's been crying.

Nina glances up. "Get Leah a drink, Si."

He stands there, paralyzed.

"What would you like, Leah?" Nina asks gently. "Tea? Coffee? Juice? A glass of wine?"

Leah gulps out something that sounds vaguely like "wine." Simon gets an open bottle from the fridge. He pours out three glasses, even though he doesn't really like the taste.

Leah drinks hers as if it's lemonade. Simon hovers. Should he stay, or go?

"Can you check what Ellie's doing?" Nina says. "And run her a bath. Keep an eye on her."

Simon's mind's racing. He strains to hear what's being said downstairs. He flips back through what happened earlier in the day, wonders if he's in trouble. For not telling Leah about the tide? For not going home with her across the fields? What if that crazy guy's followed her and attacked her or something? But he can't hear anything over the sound of the bath running.

Once Ellie's in the bathroom he goes and lies on his bed

with the glass of wine. It tastes disgusting. He leaves most of it. He turns the catalogue to the second-hand air rifles page again. There's an ad for exactly the same one as he found on the Internet, but you can send for this by ordinary mail. He'll have to get a money order from the post office.

Footsteps pad up the stairs. Simon shoves the magazine under the bed.

"OK?" Nina says from the doorway. "You look guilty!" She laughs. "Our swim was fun, wasn't it? Thanks for making me go in."

"What's Leah doing here?"

"She's all upset about something. Her parents. Arguments, and . . . well, difficult things for a young girl. Her mum's not at all well. Rita told me before. Poor Leah. She's on her own too much. I'm going to see if I can help her get a job or something."

"Like what?"

"I'll ask Rita if she needs help with daycare. Or I thought Matt might like someone—"

"*No!*" Simon blurts out.

"What's the matter?"

"Nothing." He backtracks. "But, well, why would he? He's just a teacher."

"And an artist, and living on his own. He might like help with clearing up that dusty old studio, or the house, or in the garden. He's quite an important artist, you know. He has exhibitions, and sells his paintings and sculptures. People come from all over especially to see them. You must come with me sometime and see them. You'd like the paintings."

"No," Simon says again. He can feel his neck going red.

"I mean, I already have."

"When? He didn't say!"

"Just today—by accident—I just ended up there on the bike, by mistake."

"Why didn't you say anything? You are so *odd* sometimes, Simon. I can't make you out. I've absolutely no idea what's going on with you most of the time."

She goes back downstairs. He's messed up again. She'll be in a mood.

He listens to the low murmur of voices from the kitchen, and then the back door clicks shut and the radio goes on.

Nina comes back up to tuck Ellie into bed. Fragments of story drift through the open door. "Her skin was as soft and delicate as a rose leaf, her eyes as blue as the deepest sea, but like all the others, she had no feet, and instead of legs she had a fish's tail. . . ."

Simon turns on the computer and starts up "Fighter Squadron."

He's still playing when Nina puts her head around the door. She says something.

"Turn that off, can't you?"

"What?" He pauses the game.

"I said, what did you think of Matt's work? You didn't tell me earlier." She laughs. "He's done some drawings of me. Big charcoal things. I hope he didn't show you those!"

"They were everywhere. How could I *not* see? How *could* you?"

She giggles again, like the girls at school do all the time. "You are such a funny thing. It's just a human body, you know. There's nothing wrong with that. You'll find out soon enough. You're just at that funny age."

Shut up. Go away. Leave me alone.

"Well, sorry to embarrass you, Si. But they were just drawings. You can't see anything, not really."

He hates the way she's giggling as she goes downstairs, like it's all a great joke. He turns the game on again and begins another bombing mission.

It's dark. The window's still open. Owls are calling to each other from the tall trees farther up the lane. Leah will be in her room, writing her diary like she does. He wonders briefly what her parents are arguing about. What her mother's ill with. She never talks about them.

Then he thinks about Leah, her body as she climbed out of the sea.

19

More fights. *She is getting worse. He says he's going to leave. I don't blame him really. She's been sitting in the gloom with the curtains drawn all day, not even getting out of bed, drinking herself stupid. Dad shouted because there's no food in the house again. He went down to the pub without speaking. I told Nina about everything this evening and she was really nice. She treats me like a grownup. She is going to help me get a job.*

When she mentioned Matt I nearly died. It's like she's setting us up on purpose. Perhaps he has mentioned me to her already???

I am never going to that cliff place again. I nearly drowned. If Simon hadn't come along I would have died. Simon Piper saved my life!! Well, except it was his fault in the first place for not telling me about tides and currents and stuff.

He has now seen me naked!! He could not take his eyes off me! I am so brown all over with almost no white bits any more, after today. That was the one good thing about today. If I get some more babysitting off Nina I can buy some new clothes ready for when we go up Matt's studio.

Tonight I am sleeping naked with no sheets even, as it is so hot. Imagine that, Simon!! His eyes were almost popping out of his baby skull. But he is sweet, really. I don't suppose he has ever seen a naked girl before. He is really shy and I like that he isn't pushy or anything like some older guys would be (except Matt Davies).

Ahh. Night night, diary. Sweet dreams, Simon.

Leah lies awake listening for the sound of her father coming back from the pub, but she doesn't hear him. Owls hoot from the big trees. It's well after eleven. Perhaps he's not coming back? He'll be at *Helen's*. She knows that, because of all the shouting earlier. Helen must be someone at work.

First thing the next morning, Leah gets dressed and tiptoes downstairs to listen at the door of the room where her mother sleeps these days. Silence.

The kitchen clock says nine fifteen. She'd expected it to be much earlier. She finds her mother's purse in her bag hanging on the back of the door and takes out twenty pounds. She'll get some groceries. Basics, like bread and milk and fruit, eggs, perhaps. And cheese. The kitchen smells musty. Leah opens the window and sweeps up the stale breadcrumbs scattered in a fine layer over the counter next to the toaster. As she crosses the tiled floor, her bare feet stick slightly where something has been spilled. She'll get the mop out later, after she's done the shopping and had something to eat. The trash needs emptying.

She glances at the house opposite as she comes out of her gate. She can hear Ellie's high voice, and Nina's, lower, answering her. Laughter. It stabs at Leah, that sound. All she doesn't have.

The town is already filling up with people making their

way down to the beach, or shopping, or just hanging around. Leah goes straight to the supermarket and gets what she needs. She reads the postcards in the newsagent's window advertising things for sale, or vacation rentals, or services offered or wanted. "Babysitter available." "Gardener/Handyperson wanted." "Dressmaking and Curtains by professional Seamstress." Now that Nina has talked to her about getting a job, she's thinking about it all the time. Especially what it will be like to have her own money. She's not doing gardening for anyone, mind you. Or sitting behind a register in the supermarket, or stacking shelves. No way.

The shopping bags are heavy. She rests them on the pavement while she looks in the bookshop window. There's no one in there apart from the woman at the register, who's reading a magazine and drinking coffee from a bright pink mug. Leah wouldn't mind working in there; it looks all clean and bright and not too much to do. She'd get to meet interesting people like Matt Davies. There's a book about standing stones in the window she can tell Simon about. That'll be a good reason for going over there later, and then she can talk to Nina some more.

"What the—?"

The voice startles her. Some stupid guy has walked right into her groceries, and apples are rolling out into the road. The girl with him starts picking them up, but they're all bruised and spoiled now. The guy doesn't even stop.

"Clumsy idiot!" Leah shouts at his back. He mouths off at her and his girlfriend giggles and runs off after him. The bag has split: all the groceries are spilling out. Leah crouches over it, shoving them back in. She feels like crying.

She's vaguely aware of a shadow over her, and someone helping, picking up apples. It's a man with tanned hands, a short-sleeved white shirt, blue shorts, leather boots. The realization of exactly who it is washes over her.

She doesn't want their first encounter to be like this! Crouched in a road over a bag of shopping, for God's sake, her face streaked with tears she now can't stop!

"Whoa, steady," he says. She feels his hand on her arm. The place burns, as if his touch is charged. "You all right? Ignorant yob." He hands her the bag and smiles. It's the smile she's been waiting for, for weeks now. All her life, even!

"You're Nina's babysitter, aren't you? Live next door?"

She nods. "Yes," she says, in what she hopes is a sexy, grown-up sort of voice. "I'm Leah."

"Matt Davies," he says, and shakes her hand as if it's an interview or something. Hers is much too clammy and probably sticky too. His is cool, just as she knew it would be. She notices everything, all the tiny details, like the little black hairs on the back of his hands, and his slim fingers, and the way his shirt smells of thick cotton, because she knows she will want to write them all down later so she can go over it properly in her mind. He's so close up!

"Are you going back home?" he asks. "I can give you a lift up the hill if you want. I've just got to pick up a book I ordered and then I'm going over to see Nina."

She nods. "Thanks."

Amazing! She waits for him outside the bookshop. Through the window, she watches him say something which makes the woman at the register smile, then he gives Leah a little wave and points to his watch, holding up three fingers. Three more minutes. Leah tries to glimpse her reflection in the window to check her hair. If only she'd worn something newer, not these faded denims and a boring black T-shirt. Her hair needs washing. She's not wearing any makeup at all.

"All set? I'll carry one of the bags. I'm parked up near the church. OK?"

She feels like putty. She smiles and flicks her hair, and imagines how anyone looking at them would see a man and a young woman, a couple, carrying their shopping back to the car. She can hardly believe what is happening. It's as if it's all meant to be.

He puts the bags on the back seat and holds open the front passenger door for her. She slides herself in gracefully, like a celebrity. While he's sorting himself out she has a quick look in the mirror. She doesn't look too bad.

He gets in the driving seat and turns to her. "I expect you'll be learning soon. Driving, I mean. You need to, around here."

She smiles. She wouldn't dream of telling him she's only just sixteen.

It only takes a few minutes to get back. He talks most of the way.

"Expect you'll be babysitting for Nina again? I guess the money's useful. Any plans for the summer? Mind you, you look as if you've had a month in the South of France already!"

He's noticed her tan, then. Move over, Nina!

Poor Nina. She doesn't stand a chance. But no, Leah won't let herself think like that. You've got to look out for yourself. No one else will. That's how it works. *All's fair in love and something. Play? War?* One or the other.

"Thank you very much, Matt," Leah says demurely as she gets out and retrieves her shopping bags.

He grins. "Any time. Glad to help. See you soon."

She can feel him watching her as she goes through her gate into the front garden.

Not such a bad first encounter after all.

In the kitchen, stacking the food away in the cupboards and making herself a sandwich, Leah goes over the scene again. Now she thinks of all the things she messed up: no makeup, crying over the spilled groceries, not saying anything intelligent in the car. She should have asked him about the book he was buying, or his art.

She can't go over to see Nina while he's still there, and he's there ages. She hears all their voices in the yard. Sounds like Ellie's playing with a friend. There's a strange sound coming from the house, from Simon's room. It's a sort of rhythmic *thwack thwack*. Leah guesses he's shooting something with his slingshot. What is it with him? It's as if he's always in training, practicing for an imminent attack. Must be prepared.

She looks at her own yard. It's a mess. The trash is overflowing. It's full of empty bottles. She should tidy it up. Plant things, like Nina's doing in her yard. Pots of flowers.

From having nothing to do, there suddenly seems to be too much. The house and the yard need sorting out, and she might as well do it. No one else is going to. She needs money. Maybe she should change, go across the road to see Nina while Matt is still there and ask about a job.

Leah gulps down her sandwich and goes upstairs to see if there's any hot water. Enough for a shampoo, she figures, hand on the tank in the airing cupboard. There's a funny smell in there. She shuts the door again.

By the time she's washed and dried her hair and changed into her favorite turquoise top and short denim skirt, and put her head around the door of her mother's room to check her, and finally got herself across the road to Nina's, Matt's car has gone.

20

Simon watches Leah cross the garden to where they're sitting out. He's still mad from having to be polite to Matt Davies, who sat around for much too long.

"Coffee, Leah?" Nina asks. "We've just had one, but there's enough left in the pot. Simon, get another cup out, please."

"Get it yourself."

Nina flushes, but he knows she won't make a scene in front of Leah.

"It's OK," Leah says. "I don't drink coffee. It's bad for the skin."

Nina smiles. "I like it too much to care!"

"It's an addiction," Simon says. "Caffeine's a drug."

"Just listen to him! Mr. Purity. Why so virtuous suddenly? Simon, who only drinks water—" Nina teases.

Leah joins in. "And who never touches any evil substance unless it's a can or ten of hard cider with a pal called Johnny."

Simon stares at her. She's really gone too far now. Thinking she can join in the family banter. Who does she think she is?

Nina looks shocked. She didn't know about the hard cider.

"Time I got moving," Nina says. "Did you want something in particular, Leah?"

Leah looks puzzled. She hasn't a clue what she's just done, alienating everyone.

"I was going to ask you about the job, the one at the studio? Whether you've talked to him?"

"No, but I could take you up there later, if you like. We can ask him then. This afternoon all right? And I was wondering if you'd babysit tomorrow?"

Simon's head feels like it's about to burst. Everything is running out of control—Mum, Leah, Mr. Davies. They're all getting mixed up together, and he doesn't like any of it.

"I can babysit tomorrow," he says. "I'm not going anywhere. You don't need Leah."

"Well, we'll see." Nina purses her lips. "Can you be ready about three to go to Matt's studio, Leah? We'll take Ellie and her friend too. And stop off for ice cream on the way back. It is vacation, after all."

Simon leaves them to it. They're all ganging up on him. He doesn't want to eat some lousy ice cream anyway. He stomps up to his room and sits on the floor, back against the wall. The knife that was once his dad's is lying on the floor. The leather sheath is coming unstitched along one side, but he still loves it, the way it smells authentic. You can't buy a knife like this, not even in an army surplus place. The metal handle is made up of different colored strands, red and gold and black. The blade is smooth and sharp. Dad bought it abroad somewhere on his travels. That's what Simon's going to do, as soon as he's old

177

enough: travel. Get out of this place and find some real wilderness.

He's sick of this house already. There's nothing to do. He's going to get that air rifle anyway, whatever Mum thinks. He'll go down the post office this afternoon to get the money while they're all having cream teas.

Ellie appears in the doorway. Her friend hovers behind, scared. She's seen the knife. He strokes the blade.

"Mum says, do you want lunch?"

"What is it?"

"Tuna mayo sandwiches. Or cheese."

"Nah. I'll get something later."

He goes out without saying goodbye, down to the town. After he's sent off the order for the air rifle, he wanders along Fore Street and checks out who's at the arcade. No one he knows. He walks along the beach wall. The tide's still high, so there's not much room for all the vacationers to spread out their shelters and chairs and towels and other junk. What's the point in carting all that stuff down on the beach every day anyway? People are weird. He walks up the hill to the coast path to get away from all the crowds. Sometimes he hates people. He pretends he's got his new gun and takes imaginary potshots at seagulls. He wonders what his friends are doing right now.

There's a wind today. Better for walking. He passes several people coming the other way along the path; they nod at him, or say hello in that cheery way walkers have, as if they know you. He keeps one hand on his pocket, lightly resting on the slingshot. He's not far now from the place where he first saw Mad Ed, when he asked him the way. He remembers Mad Ed's watery eyes and the way his hands shook, and how his feet shifted around all the time. Something strange about him, certainly. But did he seem mad? How would you know? It was more like he was afraid.

It's weird the way fear gets you in the guts. Or the bowels. A foul, hot sensation like you're about to shit yourself. People do sometimes, when they're really frightened. Like, about-to-die sort of frightened. Just before a plane crashes, for example. Or on the front line.

There were units stationed all along this coast in the Second World War. And prisoner-of-war camps just up the road. Secret training operations. A man at the museum told Simon that when he was a boy he and his pals used to hang over the edge of the pier, begging chocolate off US marines practicing in the bay. There are no photos of the landing craft; it was all top secret. Most of the men stationed in the town got killed in the D-Day landings.

If he keeps walking far enough, he might get to that Ministry of Defence place where Johnny says they did secret nerve-gas research. It takes him a long time. He has to go near where Matt Davies lives; he can see the roof of the studio and the house. He keeps on going.

The landscape changes. There are remnants of old mine workings, chimneys, rusting winding gear. Every so often there are traces of metal rails, grown over with grass and moss, where they must have taken the ore out on trucks. He'll explore the mineshafts sometime with Johnny and Pike and Dan. You'd need safety helmets and ropes and headlamps. It's illegal, of course.

At last he comes across signs of Ministry of Defence land. It's creepy; strangely still. Simon tries to work out what's different. That's it, there's no birds. Not even seagulls. The concrete buildings are fenced off behind rolls of barbed wire. Rusting signs say "DANGER! KEEP OUT!" The grass looks thin and barren. There are patches of this-tles and nettles, and ghostly spikes of rosebay willowherb gone to seed. The wind carries the grey thistledown in drifts.

Simon lies down on the parched earth, contemplating the scene. He lies so still, two rabbits hop out across the grass just the other side of the fence. He watches them; there's something odd about them too. They've got some sort of disease. Their eyes are swollen and too large in their heads.

Most of the windows in the main building have already been smashed. Simon picks up a stone and lobs it over the fence at the nearest window. Broken glass tinkles onto the concrete floor inside. The rabbits don't even twitch their ears. Deaf. Blind. He gets his slingshot out, loads it up with a stone. Putting them out of their misery, that's all.

But he knows that's a stupid way to think, really. Like saying you're putting an animal to sleep. It's just killing. It's a sort of selfishness. Because you can't stand to see illness or pain, and what it makes you feel. Why pretend?

And him, now? He wants the thrill of shooting some-thing. It gives him a rush of adrenalin. The feel of focused intent, absolute concentration. Power.

The first one keels over without a sound. The second one keeps nibbling the grass as if it hasn't even noticed. Simon selects a second stone, loads it, pulls back the rub-ber, aims, releases. The rabbit spins, twitching and jerking, and flops over onto its side.

Easy.

It would be much the same killing something bigger, wouldn't it? And with the air rifle even easier, once he's gotten the hang of it. Even something much bigger, say. A split-second scene flashes up before he can stop it. Motorbike. Tree. A man convulsing at the side of the road. He turns away from the rabbit corpses. He won't be taking them home to eat.

It's hard to believe this was really a research center for nerve gas. The buildings look too basic with their brick walls and regulation MOD metal window frames. Hardly the place for a laboratory. Perhaps Johnny made the whole story up. Simon climbs up a few rungs of the wire-mesh fence, just to see how easy it would be to climb over. There's barbed wire along the top, but you could cut it. Probably alarmed back then, but not any more.

Something flashes.

Simon jumps off the fence. What was it? A piece of broken glass catching the sun? A signal? A warning?

This place is beginning to get to him.

He looks around. There's nothing but grass and heather and tumbledown stone walls. And the restless sound of the sea, invisible from here. He sits back on the scruffy grass, one hand on the slingshot just in case.

Right now, Nina and Ellie and her friend Amy and Leah will be chatting together, stroking the Border collie dog up at the farm, ordering scones and cream and jam. None of them will be thinking about him. No one cares.

He tries to think about Leah in a sensible way. She's pretty, she's too old for him, he doesn't really know her, she can't really be interested in him. But there was that kiss. He can't imagine now how it could possibly have happened. Might it happen again? The only place he can begin to imagine it is there, in that deep dark chamber, where everything is different. Like being suspended in a time and sense warp. A sort of black hole.

But maybe he and Leah could go swimming again, next time the tide's right. There's no harm in that, is there? As long as Dan and Johnny and Pike are away, and no one can find out.

His nerves are on edge now. Everything makes him jump, even the tiniest rustling of grass as a mouse or shrew scurries through. No one's around for miles, as far as he can see in any direction. The walkers have all stopped for ice creams in the town, or zigzagged inland to one of the farms that do teas.

He walks along the perimeter fence, slicing off the tops of thistles with his knife. It's so sharp it cuts right through the thick stalks with one swipe. The same with nettles, and even heather and gorse. He likes the sound it makes, like a whip. He examines the blade, wipes the green sap off on his T-shirt, runs his finger along the edge. By mistake, he cuts his own skin. He feels nothing for a second, and then as he squeezes the flesh, blood begins to bead along the cut and drip down his hand and he feels the sharp stabbing pain. His hand begins to throb. He imagines Leah bending over his hand, holding it in hers. An image comes of her face, her mouth, her tongue licking the cut clean, sucking his fingers. He gives in and lets the images come, like a film sequence. X-rated.

He hears something, jerks round. Was it footsteps? A dragging sound, moving away. Someone was there, watching him. For how long? The hairs along the back of his neck bristle. It's as if he's being stalked. He's not the hunter, he's the prey.

He starts the long walk home.

Instead of going straight back, Simon finds himself taking the rutted track down to the shabby farmhouse where Mad Ed lives. He remembers the house. There was a woman—a housekeeper or cleaner or someone, he presumes now—standing in the yard that hot July afternoon when he first got scared by Mad Ed. He asked her the way.

I'll ask him. Right out. What he's doing. Following, watching . . .

Never mind that he hasn't formed the exact words yet. There is a feeling of inevitability about it. It's almost a relief to think about confronting Mad Ed. Why pretend any longer that he doesn't know who it is stalking him, even if he has no idea why?

He slows down as he reaches the farmhouse. What now? There's no car in the yard this time. No sign of anyone. Just a few chickens scratching around in the dust. No dog barking either. It occurs to him for the first time that it's odd Mad Ed doesn't ever have one with him. But a dog would give the game away. He wouldn't be able to creep around unobserved like he does, would he?

The farmhouse windows have a blank look. There's a feeling about the place of something missing. Something lonely about it, although the chickens look happy enough, healthy and bright-eyed. They're not scared of Simon; one comes right up. He kneels down, puts out his hand, and it jumps up on to his arm and then his shoulder. It feels weird, having a big feathery hen perched on his shoulder, warm and smelly. He tries to shake it off but it won't go. It clings obstinately to him with its scaly feet even when he stands up.

Footsteps.

Simon wheels around.

The hen makes a soft crooning sound in its throat.

Mad Ed's only a couple of yards away, coming closer. Simon feels the blood rush to his face. He's been caught out.

But Mad Ed's no longer the hunter. He's making a face that might be a sort of smile. "She knows you, see." Mad Ed nods towards the hen. "They've a way of knowing, birds have."

Simon feels the hair on his neck prickling. *What's he going on about? He talks garbage. Pay no attention*, he tells himself.

"Thought I'd see you here sooner or later. Once I'd worked you out. Knew you'd come, eventually." Mad Ed's voice is gravelly, like it was before. The voice of someone who hardly ever speaks. He puts his hand in his pocket and scrabbles around, as if he's searching for something. He draws out a palmful of bits and pieces of things: nylon twine, nails, a door key, an oyster shell.

Simon winces at the memory of the three shells left on his camping stuff.

Mad Ed unlocks the farmhouse door and shuffles inside. "I'll make the tea." His muffled voice just reaches Simon.

It's extraordinary. It's as if Mad Ed's been expecting him. It completely throws him. He's rooted to the spot, the stupid hen still nestled down on his shoulder. He's like some ridiculous pantomime version of a pirate—hen instead of parrot. He shakes the hen off and it starts pecking around the door. Then it goes right over the threshold into the kitchen. He can't help himself looking in after it.

It's not what he expected. Mad Ed's kitchen is surprisingly neat and tidy. A row of old-fashioned china cups hang on hooks along a shelf above one of those old white enamel sinks with a wooden draining board. There's a green and cream painted cupboard. The table is scrubbed wood—not new pine, but something greyer and older, like oak. The four chairs have been tucked in neatly. It's a room trapped in the past, a 1950s film set.

In the center of the table lies Mad Ed's shotgun, a cloth and a small canister next to it. Simon can't stop staring, even when Mad Ed starts filling up the kettle and turning on the electric cooker.

His eye goes to the window sill, to the line of things Mad Ed must have collected from the beach: pebbles, shells, a piece of blue glass. There's a row of small skulls too: mouse, bird, squirrel, and a piece of stone with the edge of a fossil. One arrowhead flint.

Goosebumps creep over Simon's skin. It's all too familiar. Too much like the shelf in his own room. And still he stands there, taking it all in, mesmerized.

On the mantelpiece a photograph in a silver frame is propped against a candlestick. He can just about make out the figures of two young men in desert khaki, leaning against a tank. Mad Ed and his brother? Before he got shot?

"Keep away, I told you," Mad Ed mutters, "but you didn't. How could you? It's where you belong, and you never meant to leave me behind, did you?"

Mad Ed's talking crazy stuff. He's mixing him up with someone else. Simon suddenly understands.

He clears his throat. It feels dry, tight. "I'm Simon," he says. "You've seen me with friends from my school, Pike and John and Dan. Pike's dad knows you."

Mad Ed turns around and stares at him, blank as anything. Then he crumples a bit, and pulls out a chair and sits down. "What do you want?" he says, his voice a rusty whisper this time.

Simon tries again. "I don't want anything," he says simply. "I'm sorry. I was just walking back this way. . . ."

It's not the truth, though, is it? He does want something. He wants to know, to understand what it is that Mad Ed's up to, following him, tracking him down along the cliffs, watching him with Leah. . . . He wants to know what's in his strange, crazy mind . . . and how he got to be like that, and how you stop it from happening . . . and about the war, and what it's really like, shooting to kill. . . .

But this is a crazy man. A headcase. There's no way of asking him any of this. Mad Ed's locked in his own mad mind. How can he possibly have answers for Simon?

Simon glances at the gun, harmless enough on the table, waiting to be cleaned.

"I'd best be going back now." Simon's voice shakes. He feels slightly sick.

There's a sudden flapping, squawking sound from a box under the table that Simon hasn't noticed before. He jumps.

Mad Ed laughs, a surprisingly normal-sounding laugh. The tension in the air shifts slightly. "He's getting better, he is."

Simon remembers the gull on the harbor wall that time with Pike.

"Is it a gull?"

"Kittiwake."

For a moment Simon and Mad Ed both watch the bird struggling in the box. Mad Ed goes over to it, lifts it out on to the floor. One wing trails.

"They've got no heart," Ed says, "to do that to an innocent bird. It's not like they wanted him for food."

Simon doesn't ask who "they" are.

The bird is flapping around the kitchen floor now, leaving white splashes of birdshit on the linoleum.

Mad Ed looks directly at Simon. His eyes look suddenly darker, sharp. "If you are going to take life," he says, "you have to learn to respect it too. Not killing for killing's sake."

Simon feels admonished. *I already know that*, he wants to say, but his throat's seized up, his heart beating too fast. *You don't need to tell me. I'm not like them. . . .*

"So, you've come back to me," Mad Ed mumbles. His eyes have that blank, haunted look again. Simon can't make out what he's saying any longer. The blood's rushing in his ears. He knows he should just run. Now. Before something terrible happens.

"Tried to protect you . . . to keep you safe . . . Danger . . ."

Odd words and phrases percolate through. Simon closes his eyes. He might be sick any minute.

Two thoughts have hit him like a gunshot: first, that when Mad Ed's looking at him like that, he isn't seeing Simon at all. He's seeing his brother, the one in the photograph. The one who died. He's seeing his past. And second, that what he, Simon, is seeing in Mad Ed is some terrible, distorted image of what he could become himself.

It's like looking into the future, hearing an echo of a life that could be his. The loner, the wild man, the one on the edge of things. The man with the gun. The hunter and the soldier . . .

No. No . . . !

Shut it out. Forget that he's seen any of this. Forget he came here, that he ever met Mad Ed . . . Shut it away and never think any of this again. . . .

He starts to run, stumbling and tripping over his own feet, across the yard and back to the path, back to the fields and the way home.

Mad Ed's voice echoes after him.

"You stay away from the guns and the killing," he calls, "and the girl who's no good. . . ."

Simon puts his hands over his ears as he runs.

21

I've got a job at Matt's house. It's all falling into place. Perhaps my luck is changing at last. I have to clean the house (kitchen and bathroom, mainly) and the studio, and once I've gotten used to it I might help when people come to buy stuff. It's only a few hours a week, but that's not the point. He is so cool and amazing!!!!

Babysat Ellie on Wednesday night. It turned out I needn't have, 'cos Simon was there, but Nina said she would still pay me as she'd promised. I didn't tell her I'd much rather be sitting in her house in any case, never mind the money! We watched a crap Second World War movie that Simon wanted to see and I read Ellie's story and we ate crisps and salsa dip that Nina left out. Nothing else happened. Simon was in a mood about something.

8 August

Today while I was cleaning the kitchen (his food cupboard is amazing; he has stuff I have never heard of, and the fridge is full of delicious things. I can help myself!) Matt asked me if he could do some sketches of me. It's for his new project which is this stone figure, really big. I wasn't a real model or anything, he just *wanted to do quick drawings while I got to work on stuff like washing up and sweeping the floor. Next time he might do my head while I'm sitting down. He will pay extra because you have to pay a life model.*

I don't think he pays Nina though. There are drawings of her all around the studio. They are very good and lifelike. Mostly back views but you can tell it's her. There are other ones which are hidden away, but I found them when I was having a snoop around when he was busy. She has let herself go! They won't be much help for his sculpture will they?

If he asks me to take my clothes off, what will I say?????

It is for art I suppose.

Nina has her hair tied up in all the drawings of her head and shoulders.

Nina is almost the same age as my mother! She is much older than Matt Davies.

Simon is still in a bad mood. In a funny way I am missing him. (What does this mean?)

Leah lifts her hair and twists it and holds it up behind her head. She rummages in a drawer for a hairclip. She turns to one side at the mirror, to admire the way it shows off her neck and shoulders. She can almost hear what Matt would say. Something about shape and line, the pool of shadow against bone.

It makes her look older. She leaves it pinned up.

She checks her stash of money saved from babysitting and the cleaning job. Almost enough for the new clothes. She's seen this top in the window of a new shop at the end of town. Black, with a real silk trim, and tiny buttons down the front. She imagines Matt's fingers unbuttoning them one by one, the feel of silk slipping over her shoulders.

"Leah?"

It's Dad. They've hardly spoken for days.

She stands at the bedroom door looking down at him through the banisters, holding her breath.

"I've got a place for your mother at the rehab unit at last. We can't go on like this."

Leah doesn't even want to think about it.

"So I need your help to pack up some of her things. Clothes, nighties, toiletries, that sort of thing. Has she got a bathrobe?"

Leah shrugs. If he doesn't know, why should she tell him?

"By three this afternoon? OK?"

"OK."

"I'll come back from work, then, and drive her over. You can come too if you want."

"No."

"Sorry it's like this. It's hard for everyone."

She stays there after he's slammed out of the front door. Later she'll go down and help her mother pack. She knows the routine. They've been through it all before. It hasn't worked. But it's a breathing space. You can't go on doing nothing forever. And maybe this time will be different.

Much later, when her father comes back from delivering her mother to the unit, Leah helps him pull back all the curtains, open the windows, let light flood back into the downstairs gloom. She strips the bed and bundles the sheets into the washing machine, vacuums the floor and carries all the empty glasses into the kitchen, stacking them in the sink.

When she goes upstairs her father is standing on the landing, pulling out piles of towels and sheets from the airing cupboard and removing bottle after bottle from the shelves where they've been hidden. He tips the contents down the bathroom sink and carries the empties outside in a cardboard box, dumps them next to the trashcan. It looks, Leah thinks, as if they've had a huge party. So many bottles! She manages to salvage one full bottle of gin before her father gets to it. It's a shame to waste it. She and Simon can take it with them to the beach.

Dad's on the phone to the person called Helen. He keeps saying the name, as if he likes the sound of it. Oh well. It seems more and more unreal to Leah, this life in a non-family. But that's all right. She's sixteen, she's making a new life for herself now. She doesn't need them any more.

She hears raised voices from across the road. She goes to the window to listen. It's Nina telling Simon off. Something about some magazine?

"I just don't understand you!" Nina shouts. "What is it all about? It's disgusting! Killing for the sake of it. For pleasure. Barbaric! How can you even think about it?"

She can't hear what Simon says in his defense, but she hears the door slam. Simon appears. He starts walking down the road.

Leah seizes her opportunity. "Simon!" she calls out from the window. "Where are you going? Can I come?"

He hesitates, looks back at her, grim-faced.

Inspiration comes. "I've got a bottle of gin," she calls softly, just loud enough for him to hear. "Let's go to the beach!"

She knows he can't resist her, even if he wants to. "Meet you at the stile in ten minutes?" she calls.

He nods curtly and walks on.

Leah unpins her hair, drags a comb through it quickly, puts on some lip gloss, and sprays perfume on her wrists. She finds a shopping bag for the bottle of gin and takes a towel from the pile on the landing. She clatters downstairs into the kitchen.

"I'm going out. See you later."

Her father barely looks up. He's reading the newspaper at the table. "Take your key," he says. "I'm off later too."

His mind is clearly on other things. He doesn't even ask her where she's going, or what time she'll be back. Still, what's new?

It's a relief to leave it all behind.

Simon is waiting at the stile. She smiles. He blushes. She knows he's pleased to see her, even though he can't tell her. She'd like to hold his hand and tell him everything about her awful family, but she won't. She decided that a long time ago.

22

Simon tries to blot out the scene at home. Nina calls him obsessive, but she's the one who goes on and on about everything. She doesn't understand anything. It doesn't mean he's evil, wanting an air rifle. It's nothing to do with the kind of films he watches. Computer games. "Macho TV shows," or whatever she said. What's she going on about? His dad would've understood. That's what he should have said. That would have shut her up.

So what will she be like if she finds the actual gun? She'll go completely nuts. It will be arriving tomorrow, probably. He'll have to ask Leah if he can hide it at her house, just till Johnny's back. She's coming down the lane now. She looks amazing.

"Hi, Simon. So, where are we going?" Leah asks brightly.

He shrugs. "Anywhere. Where do you want to go?"

"Our beach? I brought a towel. And this!" She giggles, shows him the bottle.

Simon blushes at the way she says *our*. "The tide will be too high."

"Well, I'm not in a hurry! We can wait! Let's go there

anyway and see."

"There's another cove, much farther along," Simon says. "If you don't mind walking a long way. What time have you got to be back?"

"It doesn't matter," Leah says. "You?"

"I'm already in trouble. It won't make any difference."

They climb over the stile into the tunnel of trees.

"What were you arguing about?"

"Air rifles."

Leah unscrews the bottle and they both take a swig. It burns his throat. He doesn't like it. He doesn't tell her he's never tasted gin before.

"Still," Leah says, "at least your mum cares about you. She's nice, Nina. It was good of her to get me that job. She still going out with Matt?"

He shrugs. "I suppose." *Don't think. Blank it out.*

She talks on whether or not he answers. It becomes easy after a while, just to let her go on. The air is fresher in the fields, but it's still warm. There's hardly any wind. After a while, Leah takes his arm and hangs on, and he doesn't stop her. She stops every few minutes for a swig from the bottle. They'll never get there at this rate.

"There's a mist coming in," Simon says. "Look."

It curls in over the cliff and rolls over the fields. It's surprising how quickly it comes, and how utterly it changes the look of things. He can hear the lighthouse foghorn all the way across from the bay. But it's still warm, even in the mist. They keep walking along the grass track, across the fields and over the stone stiles.

"What's that?"

There's a dark shape ahead of them, towards where the

cliff must be, although he can't see it. He can't hear the sea either.

"We must have gotten to the burial chamber already," Simon says.

"Let's go in again!" Leah says.

Does she remember what happened in there? Does she think about it at all? He can't even look at her now. She sounds so chirpy and oblivious, as if going inside doesn't mean anything to her.

She sits herself down just outside and gets the bottle out again. "Drink?" She holds it out for him.

He takes the smallest gulp he can get away with. It tastes disgusting.

"This is what my lovely mother does all day," Leah says. "She's an alcoholic." Her voice sounds suddenly bleak.

"Sorry," Simon mumbles. What else can he say?

"Well don't be," Leah snaps. She stands up and lurches forwards, into the mouth of the burial chamber.

Simon doesn't know what to do. He's not seen Leah like this before. He waits for ages, then he edges forward. He can just make her out, a dark shape within darkness, crouched over, shaking as if she's crying. Is it his fault? He goes hot.

He can't face her, not in there. He waits a bit longer, then he calls out, "Leah? Come on. Let's go to the beach."

Silence.

He peers inside again. She seems to be standing up now, in the middle of the main chamber. What's she doing? He goes in just a little way.

There's that weird sensation again, everything being sucked out of you. He can hardly breathe.

"Leah?"

She takes no notice. He stumbles forward and grabs her arm and she swings around, suddenly close up and real. It's like the time before. The muffled sound, the electric charge. A tingling sensation. He feels Leah's arms round him, squeezing him tight. He can feel her trembling. She buries her head in his chest. What should he do? But she knows, she's in charge. He feels her hand reach up and pull his head down, and then her lips, soft on his. Kissing him. He tastes her mouth, scented and sharp from the gin. He puts one hand on her back and finds bare flesh, cool naked skin. She picks up his other hand and places it right on her breast under her T-shirt. He daren't move. Can't breathe. She feels so soft and warm. *Stop thinking.* He lets his mind float off and his body take over.

Warm. Soft. Close.

Her mouth will swallow him up. Her tongue like a fish, like a slippery eel. He'll suffocate.

He surfaces for air. She tastes of gin, but her hair smells of apple. He strokes it. So soft. He's spinning, dizzy with sensation.

Leah tugs at his T-shirt, his belt. "Take them off," she whispers. She pulls away from him just long enough to drag her own top over her head. He hears the *purr* of the zip on her skirt, feels it slide over her hips. It's so dark he can see nothing, but he can feel her, naked and so warm, pressing herself against him, pulling his jeans, her hands smoothing his naked sweaty skin. He shivers with pleasure, with fear.

He half wants to stop her, to check her out. *Is this what you really mean? Is this OK? Shouldn't we think about what we're doing?* He half wants to stop and work it out for himself. *Is this what I want?* Like a deep memory, an echo, the thought comes that this matters, that it shouldn't be like this, not so silent and frantic and fumbling, but suddenly it's too late to stop, he can't, she's pushing him down with her onto the soft heap of their clothes on the earthy floor— and then it's all over. Too quick. He's trembling with shock.

Leah is making the strangest sound, half crying, half laughing, a sort of moaning, crooning sound. He slides over to lie next to her and shuts his eyes. He feels as if he is spinning off into the darkness, that he might disappear completely and forever.

By the time they stumble out into the field it's completely dark, and the mist has lifted. He can't see her expression. He's vaguely aware of her pulling her skirt straight, and brushing soil off, and then she slumps against the entrance stones and swigs from the gin bottle again. She's had way too much. How's he going to get her home now? Her speech sounds slurred. She keeps thanking him for something. He doesn't understand what. He keeps expecting her to shout at him, or swear, or run off, or *something*.

But she doesn't. None of it makes any sense to him. It's not like he'd thought it would be. Not that he's really thought about it, not actually, in detail, not happening for real. Not yet. He's not ready for any of this. It's too soon. It's all spiraled out of his control.

"You know what?" Leah keeps saying. "You're lovely, Simon."

He's way out of his depth. His head's aching. He longs to be by himself. Or with someone like Johnny, someone straightforward and undemanding, shooting crows or something simple like that.

It's not simple though, is it? What happened in there, what they did together, it was the first time, and there's only ever one first time, and it matters. It connects him with this girl, Leah, however fumbled and awkward and unintended it was.

And there was a moment in there when he felt her: warm and alive, and real, and close to him.

He hasn't felt like that before, ever.

He wishes Leah hadn't drunk so much. It spoils it. It's possible she won't even remember tomorrow. That it was all a silly drunken mistake.

"How far's it to your beach?" Leah slurs the words, giggles. "I need a swim."

"It's too far now," Simon says. "We'd better go back."

"Pull me up!" she says.

He helps her to her feet. She nearly topples over again. He has to support her with his arm round her and she leans into him. He feels her hair against his face. They make their way slowly back along the path. Leah has a faint smile on her face all the way. She stops at one of the stiles and fumbles at her wrist. "My bracelet," she says. "It's not here. Got to find it . . ."

"Not now," he says. "You'll never find it now in the dark. It could be anywhere. We'll come back and look another time."

Now that the mist has lifted, the sky is completely clear, studded with millions of stars. There's Orion, hunter, the three bright stars at his belt. And the Big Dipper, and Sirius. And a bright planet: Mars, perhaps.

Night navigation. Finding your way at night. He knows the pages of the survival guide almost by heart. But there's no page for where he is now, no guide from this point.

At Leah's gate, she turns and hugs him tight. Her house is all in darkness. In his, there's one light on upstairs: his mother's room. She's waiting to see that he's safely back.

He watches Leah stagger inside.

Such a night.

He creeps upstairs in his own house and shuts his bedroom door. No way can he let his mother see him.

He lies on the bed, exhausted.

So many stars.

Galaxies of them.

Three thousand years ago, when the huge stones for the burial chamber were being hewn and hefted, they would have been just the same stars.

23

The first thing he thinks of when he wakes up is the burial chamber, and what happened. His body goes hot all over, remembering. He can still smell her, the sweet scent of her hair and the bitter smell of gin. He thinks about how soft she felt. How in some way she needed him.

It comes to him like a sudden revelation, how lonely she really is.

He hears a van draw up outside, and a voice. The mail! He pulls on a pair of jeans and rushes down to get there before anyone else sees. The postman is getting a long box out of the van.

"I'll take it," Simon says.

Lucky or what! He lugs it back to his room. It's heavy. But that's not the reason his heart's hammering in his chest like that. He pushes the box under his bed, even though he'd like to rip it open and have a good look straightaway. Better to wait till he knows where everyone is, when they're all safely out of the way.

Ellie's in the front room watching TV. Nina still seems to be in bed. Her door's closed. It must be earlier than he thought. He showers, finds clean clothes, combs his wet hair, studies himself in the mirror. Not too bad. He runs his hands through his hair to mess it up again. Better.

By the time he gets downstairs Ellie and Nina are in the yard. Nina doesn't say anything about how late he was last night. Nor does he. He makes toast and takes it out to the table under the tree.

"We're going to a new beach today," Ellie says. "And we're having supper with Matt."

Nina's watching his response. *Careful.*

"Do you want to come to the beach?" Ellie asks. She snuggles up close to him on the bench and he lets her, for once.

"Where?" he asks.

Ellie doesn't know.

"Portheras Cove," Nina says. "It's supposed to be beautiful. Want to come?"

"I don't think so," Simon says cautiously.

"But you'll come for supper?"

"Do I have to?"

"Yes."

"Well, then. Yes, I guess."

"Good. Since he's invited us all specially."

"What time?"

"Seven thirty? We'll make sure we're back from the beach by six. What will you do? You seeing Leah?"

"No," Simon says. *Has she guessed? Did she see them coming back last night? What would she say if she knew what he'd done?*

"We'll take a picnic, Ellie. Want to help?"

Simon watches them go into the kitchen together. He hears them chatting easily together as they make sandwiches. They seem a million miles away.

Two secrets now: the air rifle and Leah. It's like he's moved on to a completely different planet, and they've absolutely no idea.

When they've gone to the cove, he gets the box out and spreads the different pieces on the bed. There's an instruction sheet about how to fix on the scope using special mounts, and how to line up the scope using the adjusters. The gun's got a silencer. His heart beats fast all the time. He strokes the smooth wooden stock, practices holding it steady at his shoulder, flicks the safety catch. He reads everything it says about safety and dangers. How never to carry the gun loaded. Always keep the safety catch on. Carry it barrel down.

Nina would have a complete fit if she saw him now. He has never so openly defied her. There's no going back now.

One canister of lead pellets was in the box with the air rifle. He pours some into his cupped hand and examines them closely. Each one is a tiny mushroom shape, with a curved top.

He examines the rifle slip for carrying the gun. It's in good shape. You can't tell any of it is secondhand.

He makes a set of cardboard targets. He can set them up in the garden, since no one will be back till six, and practice shooting.

It goes well. Over a couple of hours, he definitely gets better. It's more difficult than he expected, though, to aim right. He gets used to the feel of the rifle jerking as it fires, the way your body absorbs the energy.

He gets it all tidied up and away by three, just in case

they're back early from the beach. He hides the air rifle in its slip in the box, wrapped around with an old sheet, pushed well under the bed. He'll ask Leah sometime whether he can keep it at her house. If she's still speaking to him.

He hasn't seen her all day. There's no sign of anyone being in. She's sleeping, maybe. Sleeping off a hangover. Avoiding him? Or she could have gone out when he was shooting. He wouldn't have heard anything, then. What will he say when he sees her? What if she doesn't even remember what happened? He doesn't even want to think about it right now. It's been a relief, just focusing entirely on the air rifle.

The next hours drag. He turns the radio on while he makes a sandwich. It's tuned to Radio Four, and he catches the end of a documentary program about scientific experiments on soldiers without them knowing. They mention the nerve gas sarin. Old men talk about what happened to them. How they thought they were being injected with the common cold virus. Now they're getting cancers and muscle-wasting diseases. Next there's a news bulletin. Two more Americans shot in Iraq. A bomb on a bus in Israel. A seven-year-old boy recovering in the hospital after being swept out to sea on vacation somewhere.

He wishes he'd gone to the beach now. It's too hot.

At last he hears the car.

Ellie runs up. "We went in the sea and I swam without armbands! There was a real live starfish on the sand and we put it back in the water. And there was a dead jellyfish!"

Over her head, Simon sees Leah get out of the car and go into her house without waving or looking at him. His heart starts to thud.

"Simon?" Ellie tugs at him again. He wasn't listening. *What was Leah doing in the car?*

Nina closes the car door and smiles at Simon. She dumps a pile of sandy towels on the path. "OK, Si? We had a lovely time. Almost too hot on the beach. But it's perfect for swimming. You should've come."

"Did *she* go with you?" He can't say her name out loud.

"Who? Leah?" Nina glances over to the house. "No! We just gave her a lift back from the bus stop. She's been at work, at Matt's. Anyway, I'll just rinse this stuff out and hang it out to dry and then we can start getting changed and ready to go out. I need a shower."

Simon scowls. Changed into what? And why?

He goes up to his room and lies on his bed with his eyes shut. He thinks of his new gun hidden underneath.

He's in a forest in Kamchatka, far east Russia. Forest makes up seventy percent of Russian territory. It spans twelve time zones. The lungs of Europe. Night's closing in. He hasn't eaten for days. But he's been following the tracks of a wild boar for hours and it's just ahead of him, crashing through the undergrowth. Now's his chance. He crouches, waits. His feet are numb with cold, but he hardly notices. His eyes strain through the dimming light. He flips the safety catch. Aims at the dense undergrowth. Waits, senses movement, fires. The animal squeals, runs, stumbles, falls, its huge weight crashing to the ground. Blood seeps onto the forest floor.

"Bathroom's free," Nina calls. "Have a shower and put on those new trousers and a clean T-shirt."

He builds a fire, ready to spit-roast a leg of the wild boar. He'll have to hang the rest in a tree, out of the way of other predators. The meat juices will run between his teeth. He'll tear the flesh from the bones.

She hammers on the door. "Didn't you hear? Hurry up."

Simon yawns. Opens his eyes. Sun slants through the window on to the dusty floor of his room. He sighs.

Matt Davies serves up oven-roasted organic chicken and Mediterranean vegetables with lemon couscous. Nina's highly impressed, Simon can see. Ellie's taken in too. She's allowed lemonade in an expensive wine glass, and doesn't have to eat any of the zucchini.

"They're all homegrown, the vegetables," Matt says.

"What, even the red peppers?" Simon says, to trip him up.

"Yep. And the eggplants. In the greenhouse. You can go and see, if you like, while I clear up here and get the dessert."

It's a good enough excuse to leave the table. Ellie gets down with him and they go out into the yard.

The stone walls trap the heat from the day. Even the paving slabs feel warm. The greenhouse door is wide open. Tiny red and green tomatoes are growing on vines in earthenware pots along one side. On a shelf are pots of pepper plants with shiny dark leaves, an eggplant, cucumbers, and a pumpkin plant. It smells amazing, a pungent, earthy smell. Ellie loses interest pretty quickly and wanders back outside to look for ladybirds. Simon stands in the green light of so many leaves, watching her. She's content, doesn't mind the way Matt soft-talks Nina, flatters her. He can hear their voices from the kitchen. He's grilling the dessert he's made, to caramelize the topping, and setting out coffee cups. Nina laughs at something he's said. She laughs a lot more these days.

The door to the studio is open. Simon wanders inside, runs his hand along the wooden bench under the window, picks up different tools. He runs the edge of the chisel over the back of his hand to feel the rasp on his skin. A stack of paper is propped up on an easel. He knows he shouldn't, but it's like a compulsion he can't resist, to lift the cover and start examining each drawing. Each one is more damning than the one before. To begin with, it's his mother in varying degrees of undress, and that's bad enough. He flicks the pages over more quickly. Mostly it's her back view, her head and shoulders, the curve of her spine. But then there are new drawings, quick charcoal sketches, a few in oil pastels which have smudged where one page falls over another. It's Leah. Leah leaning over the sink, with her hair falling in sunlight. Leah reaching up to put cups on the hooks on the cupboard. Leah sweeping the kitchen floor, Leah at the doorway, a half smile on her face. And the last one: Leah with her hair held up in one hand, showing her long neck, the curve of a bare shoulder, the line of her spine drawn so carefully you can see where each bone lies just under the skin.

He wants to throw up.

He lets the pages drop back under the cover. He'd like to kick the easel over, stamp the drawings into the dust. But Ellie is standing at the doorway, watching him.

"What are you doing?" she asks, so innocently that he can't speak. Absurdly, tears spring into his eyes and he has to turn away to blink them back.

"Mum says, are you coming for dessert and do you want

coffee?"

He's spinning, dizzy. The air in the studio is suffocating, full of stone dust. He hadn't noticed it before, but now it seems to fill his lungs and his eyes and he can hardly breathe. He stumbles past Ellie into the yard. That's when he sees the stone sculpture. It's the one Matt Davies was working on before. Emerging from the block of stone are the head and torso of a woman, only she's changing. Where her legs would have been before, he can now see the curve and slope of a fleshy fish tail, the stone surface scalloped into scales.

The head is wrapped in a soft cloth, so Simon can't see the actual features. The hands, what he can see of them, are the small, fine hands of a young woman.

He might actually be sick. Any minute.

"Si?"

He feels Ellie's small hand touching his. "Are you all right?"

"Yes," he croaks. "It was too stuffy in there."

She sits next to him on the low wall without speaking. Eventually he leans down and picks up a handful of small stones from the path. "Want to play? See if we can hit the flower pot next to the wall. The one with the red flowers in it."

Ellie crouches down to gather her own pile of stones. She looks happy again. It doesn't take much. He lets her stand closer to the pot, to make it more fair. She's still hopeless; all her stones go wide.

He hits every time. Each throw's a little harder. Eventually, he cracks the pot.

Ellie gasps and giggles. "You'll be in trouble."

"Who cares?"

She giggles again, but nervously. "Should we go and have dessert?" she asks.

"You can. I'm staying out here. Find out when we're going home and come and tell me."

There's no way he's going back in there. Or speaking to that man, ever. He'd like to smash that stupid statue thing into tiny pieces.

To think of Matt Davies, watching Leah like that, drooling over her as he draws and sculpts. And what about Nina? How's she supposed to feel?

Simon can't bear it, the muddle of it all. How it makes him feel. Sick and angry, and wretched. A horrible, messy, confusing feeling he can't explain even to himself.

He imagines blasting the stupid thing with his air rifle. Splatting it with lead shot. It's just fantasy to begin with and then it dawns on him: he could actually do it, for real. No one would know it was him. No one even knows he's got the gun.

Every time he thinks of Leah with Mr. Davies, he gets this awful ache deep in his guts, so bad it's like he's going to throw up.

He hears footsteps behind him, but doesn't turn round.

"What's the matter with you?" Nina hisses at him. "How rude can you be? Get back inside and make an effort. Now."

"No."

She grabs his arm, but he shakes her off. He's stronger than her now.

"Simon, I'm warning you. Now. I mean it."

"Warning me of what?"

"How dare you speak to me like that! All I'm asking for is decent manners. We haven't even finished the meal. He's gone to a lot of trouble, cooking special things. The least you can do is come and make some sort of conversation. We're not going until you do."

"You can't make me."

She looks as if she's about to explode, but Matt's shadow appears, and Nina turns to face him instead.

Simon listens to the low voices.

"What's up?"

"I'm sorry, Matt. He's being . . . difficult. Pigheaded. I don't know why."

Matt laughs. "It doesn't matter. Leave him there for a bit."

"It does matter. I hate it. It's spoiled your lovely meal."

"No it hasn't! And I understand. It's bound to be hardest for him. That age. Don't worry about it."

"I do worry. I hate him being so rude. Not speaking."

"That's fourteen-year-old boys for you."

"Is it? Is it *really*? And *why*? They're not all like that. He used to talk all the time when he was little. I just don't understand."

"No. You wouldn't. But I remember it only too vividly."

"What, you? You weren't like that, I bet."

"I was fourteen, wasn't I? You don't ever forget how hard it is. Finding a way through. Survival, anyway you can."

Simon puts his hands over his ears. It's even worse, listening to him being *understanding*. Better to have him and Nina angry, and then he can just hate them.

They go back inside. He hears music coming through

the open windows. It's getting dark in the garden. Moths circle closer to the lit windows. Some insect with small quivery wings brushes against his arm. A fox barks.

Nina stands at the back door, Ellie in her arms. She calls to him.

"Can you unlock the car? Ellie's asleep. Time to go."

He stands up awkwardly, stiff from sitting in one place for so long. He takes the key from her and goes ahead out of the gate. The grass is wet with dew. Matt does not come out to see them off. Nina drives home in silence. Neither of them speaks when they get back either, except for the strictest of functional purposes.

"Key."

"Carry this."

"Lock the back door."

Nina doesn't even say goodnight.

24

Simon wakes late. His room's too hot. The sun's been shining through the uncurtained window for hours. The house is quiet. He listens for evidence of what Nina and Ellie are up to, but there's nothing except a tap dripping in the bathroom. He dozes a bit longer. Images from last night bubble up to the surface. The drawings. The mermaid woman emerging from the stone.

In daylight, it all takes on a slightly different shape. It's what artists do, isn't it? Drawings from life. It doesn't mean anything significant. Leah just happens to be around while he's working. It's not surprising he's used her as a model. Same with his mother.

He thinks of himself as an artist sometimes. It's his best subject at school. But he hasn't drawn anything since this Matt Davies thing with Mum. How can he do GCSE Art now?

What he used to like about drawing was the feeling of intense absorption in something, how you get into a different state, almost like a trance. But he's discovered that you can get almost exactly the same feeling when you're hunting. You're so focused on your prey you forget everything else, even pain. He and Johnny, Pike, and Dan talked about it once when they were stalking pheasants near Pike's house. They could've gone on for hours. They crawled through brambles and stinging nettles and gorse and didn't even notice they were being scratched and stung and bruised until afterwards.

It must be some sort of adrenalin rush. Same as people who do sports. It's addictive. Afterwards, when you come back down, you feel wiped out.

There's a note propped against the butter dish on the kitchen table: *Ellie and I gone to Rita's for coffee.*

Sounds as if she's still mad at him.

He pours himself a bowl of cereal and spoons golden syrup on top. He can get the air rifle out in a minute, set it up, go over to the fields, and practice shooting for real while Nina and Ellie are out.

There's a tap at the back door. It opens. Leah stands there.

She's so . . . so golden and vibrant and alive! Nothing like the stone carving. It's the first time he's seen her, on her own, since they . . . they did that stuff. He doesn't know what to say.

She smiles. "Do you want to go out?"

His heart gives a little jolt. "Where?"

"You can choose. I've made a picnic."

He thinks of the air rifle, the smooth wood, heavy against his shoulder. Lets it go. Leah is wearing her short denim skirt and the skimpiest of T-shirts. How can he possibly resist?

His stomach flips.

"It's so *hot*!" Leah says, leaning against the door. "We

213

could go to that swimming place, the one we never made the other night?" She giggles.

She's *flirting* with him!

"Get a towel," she says, "and I'll go and get the picnic. Is Nina there?"

"No."

"Leave her a note, then, so she doesn't worry."

"Bossy," Simon says. But he does write a note. He doesn't mention Leah.

"It's too hot to walk far," Leah announces when they're only a short distance down the road. She hasn't touched him, or mentioned the other night. He wonders whether she remembers *anything*. Should he say something?

He doesn't.

"Let's go up on the cliffs instead," Leah suggests.

He follows her. His head feels muzzy, as if he can't think straight about anything.

She branches off away from the coast path once they get there and finds them a grassy patch big enough to lie down on, hidden in the tall bracken fronds. It's sheltered on one side by the remains of an old stone field boundary. Simon wonders fleetingly whether she's been here before. With someone else. *Matt Davies?* But he's not going to think about that now.

They lie side by side, him on his back and Leah on her stomach. She studies the old stones in the wall as if she's never looked at them close up before.

"Look at these plants," she tells Simon. "They're like the seaweedy stuff growing in those rock pools we saw. All different color fronds."

"Lichens," Simon says. "Only grow where the air's unpolluted. Depending where they are, you can tell which direction is north. . . ."

"*You!* All your facts!" Leah pounces on him, play-fights. They end up face to face, so close that she has to kiss him, and this time he kisses her back. He's beginning to get the hang of it. Like it, even. No one can see them here. They don't do anything else, just lie and soak up the heat, and occasionally Leah makes observations about things she sees, like the way the grass isn't just one kind of plant, but hundreds of different kinds. Some have tiny flowers like stars. Simon's about to tell her which ones are edible in a survival situation, but stops himself just in time. He's learning that too: what you say, what you don't.

"Hungry?" Leah doles out sandwiches. The chocolate cookies are so melted they suck the chocolate off each other's fingers.

Simon watches a flock of small brown birds alight, peck at the grass, then all fly off together and land a bit farther on. He doesn't recognize them. He can see kittiwakes wheeling off the cliff if he sits up. And there are the usual gulls. Voices drifting from the town beach sound almost the same as the gulls: shrieks and cries, carried on the breeze. He lies on his back, resting his head on his hands. Leah's still on her tummy, close to him. He can feel the warmth of her leg next to his. She tickles his face with a grass stem until he laughs. "Stop it!"

"It's a test," she says. "See how long you can stay still."

She tickles his eyelids, his cheek, the tip of his nose. She runs the fine grass along his top lip. He splutters, sits up, pushes her off.

"You lost!" She pushes him back down and leans over

him, her hair tickling him now, and runs her finger along his lips.

He sighs. "Don't," he begs. "Please. It's too much."

"Too much what? Pleasure or pain?"

"Both."

He'd like to ask her what she remembers about the other night in the burial chamber. He doesn't quite dare, in case she remembers nothing. He's beginning to doubt himself. Perhaps he made the whole thing up, just by wanting it.

"I might take the air rifle out later," he says.

"I heard you out in your yard yesterday," Leah says. "What do you want it for, anyway?"

"It's fun," Simon says. "And it's a skill, hunting. People have always done it. It's natural."

Leah screws up her nose. "Not any more. And it's *men*, not *people*."

"And the women just ate nuts and berries, I suppose? You eat meat, don't you?"

Leah yawns.

He can't be bothered to argue with her.

He listens to the murmuring sound of the sea. It's dead calm today; there's just the tiniest of swells. And so blue. Above them, the sky is blue too, endless. The sun's hot, but up here on the cliffs there's just enough breeze. It's almost perfect. Leah's body lies close to his, companionably. There's no need to speak.

"We could go along to the rope cove," Simon suggests when it's too hot to lie in the sun much longer.

He's imagining them both stripped off, swimming in

the cove, larking about. Drying out on the rock ledges side by side, kissing, touching each other.

Leah sits up, stretches, looks in the direction of the town beach. "I'll meet you there later," she says. "There's something I need to get in town. I forgot, earlier."

"Do you have to? Now?"

"The shops will shut at five. It won't take long. An hour, maybe? You could come too?"

He hates shops.

"I'll go along and wait for you there," he says. "Which way will you come?"

"The quicker one. Field path? Then I can drop stuff off home first."

Don't let it spoil the day, he thinks. *Sometimes things are better if you wait for them.*

He watches Leah pick her way through the bracken back on to the coast path and toward the town. He can hear her feet for a long time, click-clacking along the path. He props himself up on his elbows to see better.

Not that far away, a small group of guys in wetsuits are clambering up one of the stacks that juts up out of the sea. They climb right to the top, nearly to the edge. Simon's heart hammers just watching. One steps forward, yells, and jumps. Simon has to close his eyes. A huge splash echoes out. He opens them. The boy's head surfaces, he swims back, starts climbing the stack again. A second boy takes his turn on the high ledge. Even from this distance, Simon's pretty sure it's Rick Singleton. He doesn't jump, he does a near-perfect dive, slicing into the water. The other boys cheer. A third steps forward.

They must be crazy, Simon thinks, *jumping from there,*

with such a narrow channel of sea, and so many rocks. They could kill themselves so easily. One false move.

Simon lies back on the warm grass. Should he have gone with Leah? But he loathes shopping.

When she arrives at the rope cove, when they've swum, he'll ask her about the other night. He will.

In a minute he'll start walking along the cliff.

As soon as he gets there he realizes the tide's going to be too high for swimming. He swings down the rope anyway. He's a commando soldier, one of the free-climbing unit. He's seen the plaque on the cliff in memory of the Commando Cliff Assault Unit who trained along here in the Second World War. They came in special boats called dories.

Once he's down he pokes around in the rock pools. Every so often a wave hits the ledges and sends spray shooting over the edge. He remembers the father and son swept off rocks while they were fishing.

He's thirsty. Perhaps Leah will bring something to drink. Alcohol's no good though, it just dehydrates you more. She drinks too much. He remembers what she said about her mother: *She's an alcoholic.* It must be really hard on Leah. And that must be what Rita and Nina were going on about way back, when they called her *poor Leah.*

There's a way you can turn saltwater into fresh by making a solar still, but you need plastic, or a tarpaulin.

Leah's taking ages. It must be more than an hour.

He catches a shrimp with his hands. Fish dart under rocks. He feeds the shrimp to a sea anemone at the edge of the rock pool. Anemones look like flowers, but they're not.

They are carnivorous.

She's not going to come, is she? She's changed her mind. It was just an excuse, the shopping thing. She was bored with him. He's too young for her.

Eventually he has to give up. He goes home the long way, along the cliff, and swims off Gull Rock at the edge of the town beach. The sea's a deep turquoise green. Freezing. It never warms up here. He stays in as long as he can, till his teeth are chattering and his fingers blue.

When he's back on the beach, toweling himself dry, the gang of boys in wetsuits swagger past. Simon braces himself. But Rick just nods. "All right?"

Simon nods back. "All right."

Something's changed. His heart's not thumping any more. He watches Rick's retreating back. He wonders fleetingly what happened between Rick and Mad Ed that time out on the cliff.

In any case, Rick's moved on. New interests. Diving. New girlfriend.

That's what happens. Nothing ever really stays the same.

Back home, Nina's putting supper on the table. She's made enough for him.

"Good swim?" she asks.

"Yes."

"Water's still cold, isn't it? In spite of all the sun."

"You need a wetsuit, really. Everyone has them."

"We could get you one, if you like."

Her peace offering.

"Thanks."

"What about the surfing school? Keep you busy till your friends get back?"

"Nah."

"Why not?"

"It's school, isn't it? And this is vacation."

"Si! Don't be daft. It's completely different from school!"

"I wouldn't know anyone."

Nina sighs.

"Oh yes," she adds after a while. "Nearly forgot. Leah was here looking for you."

He keeps his eyes on his plate. "When?"

"Half an hour ago, maybe?"

He finishes eating, pushes his chair back. "I'll see what she wanted."

"Can I come?" Ellie asks.

"No."

Leah is out in her yard, trying to cut the grass with blunt shears. She looks up as he crosses the road.

"You didn't come."

"I'm sorry, Si. I came over to explain, but you weren't there. It just got too late. I've got to work this evening. Matt's coming over to pick me up at seven. I bumped into him in town." She smiles. It's supposed to make him feel better. It doesn't.

"What sort of work?" he asks.

"Modeling. For the new sculpture? You know?"

He does.

He turns abruptly away. He feels sick.

"Simon?"

He starts walking back.

"Don't be like that."

He doesn't reply.

"Don't go all moody on me. I said I was sorry about the swim. I'll come tomorrow?"

He swings around. "No."

"Why not?"

"I'm busy."

"Doing what?"

"Stuff." He bangs the gate shut behind him.

"What, playing soldiers? Firing guns? Grow up, Simon."

The words echo around in his head.

Grow up. Grow up. Grow up.

Nina looks up from her book. "What did she want?"

"Nothing."

"Si?" Nina's voice is hesitant. "With Leah—just be a bit careful. It's nice that you're friends . . . she's on her own too much . . . but she's a bit of a mixed-up kid . . . problems—"

Simon stomps upstairs before she's even finished her warning speech. He shuts the door firmly, pulls the bed in front of it so no one can get in.

He turns on the computer, selects a game, turns up the volume so he won't be able to hear when Matt Davies's car pulls up to collect Leah at seven. "Stealth Squad Combat." "War Zone II." "Death Ray."

When everyone's gone to bed, he gets the air rifle out again, strokes it. He holds it up to his shoulder, aims it at the window and imagines what it would be like, blasting Matt Davies's stupid stone sculpture into a million fragments. Into dust.

25

It's late again when he wakes up. Each day of the holidays it seems to get later. He never used to sleep in like this, but he feels exhausted, weighed down by the stone in his guts.

Ellie has already gone out with her friend. Nina's getting ready to go downtown.

"Will you be all right?"

"Of course," he snaps.

"Only a week or so and Johnny'll be back, won't he? And then Dan. I'm sorry we haven't had a vacation, Si. You understand why, don't you? What with moving and everything."

"Yes. Stop going on about it."

"We ought to talk, Simon. About what happened the other night. About me and Matt. Your behavior—"

He groans out loud. He didn't mean to, it just came out spontaneously.

Nina does her tightlipped face all the time she's getting ready and slams the door when she goes.

Once she's safely out of the way, he gets the air rifle out from under the bed again. She'll be gone for ages; she's meeting her friend Tessa for lunch. Tessa used to live next door to them. She used to babysit Simon when he was little. She helped Nina through the really dark days after Dad died. She's nice. Maybe she'll talk some sense into her about Mr. Davies.

He reads the instruction book again. Then he makes some more cardboard targets.

This time, instead of the usual concentric circles with a bull's-eye, he draws animal shapes on the card: a wild boar, a deer, a rabbit with a stupid expression. Feeling suddenly inspired, he draws Matt Davies's head and torso on one of the pieces of cardboard.

He takes the targets out into the yard and arranges them against the wall at the back, out of sight of the road. He takes potshots. It makes a hell of a noise. Perhaps it's not such a good idea. He doesn't want the neighbors complaining to Nina and her finding out. He gathers up the targets. Mr. Davies has a hole in his mouth and another in the center of his forehead. Simon's getting better at aiming the shot.

It's incredibly hot again. He lies in the shade under the plum tree and dozes. He tries not to think about Leah. There's no sign of her at her house. The afternoon drags. He watches a load of crap on television. When Nina gets back she makes them both iced lemonade with real lemons. She's obviously trying to be nice. Tessa must have talked some sense into her.

The air feels sticky, thick. Flies buzz around him, stupid, irritating ones that he can't seem to swat. He read somewhere that flies have so many lenses in their eyes they can see you coming a mile off.

"Could be the South of France," Nina says for the millionth time from her deckchair under the tree. "Tessa's going on vacation there in September. With her new boyfriend. Manfriend. Lover. Whatever you call him. There isn't a right word, is there, once you're over a certain age!"

As if he was the slightest bit interested.

"We'll eat later, yes? When it's cooled down a bit?"

"I'm not hungry."

Just after seven, a car draws up. Simon watches from his bedroom window. It's Matt Davies's car, but he doesn't come to their house to see Nina. Leah comes out of her house, all dolled up in some black low-cut thing, and jeans that barely cover her butt. Her hair's tied up differently.

Simon's limbs feel weak. He watches the way she smiles at Mr. Davies, the way he holds the door open for her. She gets in the front seat next to him. He drives off.

Inside him there's a hard knot pulling tighter.

He's about to go downstairs when he sees his mother standing at the front room window, very still. He feels guilty, as if he's witnessed something private, something he shouldn't have. He creeps quietly back into his room and closes the door.

From a prone position on his bed he blasts Matt Davies and Leah Sweet with automatic rifle fire, like in all the best movies. He plays with the scenario in his mind, trying different versions. A car chase and then a shootout. A car chase and then a dramatic cliff-top plummet onto rocks below, a fireball. Miraculously, Leah walks out alive.

In most of the scenes, everyone dies.

Another car draws up. He goes to look. But it's just Amy's mum bringing Ellie home. When he goes downstairs to find something to eat he finds Nina and Ellie snuggled up in front of the TV watching some tedious house-makeover show. Ellie's not interested, obviously, but it's a good excuse to cuddle up with Nina and stay up later than usual. He knows; he used to do it himself.

The house has absorbed heat from the sun all day. Even though the windows are wide open, there's no air. Moths beat their soft wings against the lampshades, fatally drawn by the light. They can't help themselves, it's what they're programmed for. To follow the light of the moon. They don't know it's just a forty-watt light bulb that will scorch their wings and burn them up if they get too close.

Simon doesn't tell anyone he's going out. They're so absorbed in the television, nestled up close and cozy, it's easy to smuggle the air rifle downstairs and out to the shed. He gets himself organized: the air-rifle slip has a strap so he can wear it on his back and keep his hands free for the bike, though it will be harder to balance. He feels it there, heavy and protective, like a shield. Like a crab's shell. He pushes the bike through the yard out into the road and gets on.

No one sees him go.

26

He hasn't really planned it out. He's not thinking at all. He's just got to see with his own eyes. Got to do something, to stop the muddle going around and around in his head.

It takes ages, biking up the hill and all the way along by the moor. He's forgotten his lights, but it doesn't really matter because there are no cars and there's a golden moon rising, so bright it casts shadows.

He leaves the bike half hidden in the hedge at the top of the track leading down to the house and the studio. He takes the air rifle with him, still slung on his back and banging against his legs as he walks. The air feels damp: dew, or a sea mist moving in over the cliff, the way it does sometimes after a really hot day. He walks down the middle of the track on the scrap of scruffy grass and weeds which deaden his footsteps. No one must know he's here.

If he lived way out like this he'd have a dog. But it's just as well Matt Davies doesn't have one. It would be barking by now. They have amazing hearing, hundreds of times better than humans.

The lights are on in the house, the windows wide open.

He can hear music: jazz or blues. *Grownup* music.

Simon shivers. His scalp prickles. His limbs feel heavy. He creeps forward more slowly now, ducks down as he reaches the yard wall. He stays low, edging along and around the end wall that encloses the yard, so that he ends up off the track, on the rough land that runs between the yard and the cliff. No man's land. His senses are on full alert.

At this end of the yard the wall is much higher. He can stand up without being seen from the house. There's a ditch along the bottom of the wall, which must fill with water in the winter. The grass is longer here.

The air stinks of rotting grass clippings. The compost heap must be just the other side of the wall, behind the greenhouse. He detects another, ranker smell: fox. Every so often other smells waft over the wall: honeysuckle, sweet-peas. And the chalky, dusty smell of the studio.

He's holding his breath.

Clink clink. What's that? The chinking, chipping sound of metal against stone. A light's on in the studio. Matt Davies is working, then. Simon can't hear any voices, just the music from the house. Perhaps Leah has already gone home.

Simon's heart is beating fast, like a bird's when you hold it in your hand. They rescued a sparrow once from a cat, when Simon was little. His dad showed him; you could actually see the heart beating through its feathers, it was that terrified. He put out his hand and felt the tiny, speeding flutter. They put the bird in a box and gave it food and water, but it died anyway.

Simon clambers up the rough wall, feeling for footholds

in the stone, until he can see over the top. Matt Davies is silhouetted against the studio light, working just outside on the covered area, chipping away at the stone figure. The cloth has been removed, but it's too far away for Simon to make out the details of the face, if it has one.

There, farther into the garden, is Leah, sitting silently on a chair, turned to one side. Her hair is loose now, twisted roughly over one shoulder to leave the other bare. And in the blend of artificial light from the studio and the moonlight, Simon can see perfectly well that down to the waist she is naked. She sits so still she might be made of marble or stone herself. He watches her, entranced. How extraordinarily beautiful she is. How perfect her body, its curves and hollows.

A low voice says something. Leah laughs and shifts slightly. The spell is broken. She is flesh and blood after all.

Simon watches on, hidden in the deep shadow at the edge of the garden, heart fluttering like the injured bird.

Matt puts down his chisel. He stretches, as if he's tired after concentrating for a long time. He turns, picks something up, chucks it towards Leah. It's her black top. Simon watches her slowly button it up. Leah stands up and yawns, says something, moves towards the open kitchen door. Matt clears away his tools, turns off the studio light and follows her into the house.

Simon is shaking all over. He sits back on the damp grass.

How could she? Matt Davies is more than twice her age.

I mean nothing to her.

That night meant nothing. I'm just a kid. That's what she said, didn't she? "Grow up, Simon!"

And what about Nina? How can Leah be so mean? She's just used her to get what she wants. Stealing her boyfriend . . . The word makes him wince.

As for Mr. Davies: what does he think he's playing at? I used to like him. As a teacher, at least. Respected him. Thought him interesting, fair, a good guy.

Simon feels hollow with disappointment. And each single disappointment is tucked inside another. His friends. Nina. Mr. Davies. Leah. Like that Russian doll Ellie has that you undo to find another inside, and then another, down to the tiny one in the middle of it all. In the middle of him it feels as if there's just a cold hollow space.

This is how it happens, he thinks. *This is how you stop yourself feeling so much. You go cold, colder still with each small disappointment, each betrayal, until you find you've frozen over at the core of you, and you stop feeling anything anymore.*

He watched this film on television not long ago, about what they do to harden you up for the army. A systematic, brutal stripping-away of your individuality, of everything that's warm, and feeling, and human. One humiliation after another. He knew even while he was watching it, fascinated, that it was crap. And yet even when his mother had stormed out of the room in disgust he'd watched on, unable to tear himself away, knowing that this was what happened for real. There was a truth he was witnessing. And it isn't just in the army. It's everywhere. *Making a man of you.* That "women and children first" crap which only means that men's lives matter less. That's what you have to believe if you're going to send armies of them into wars.

Blinding rage at the injustice of it all begins to unwind from where it's been coiled in the pit of his belly for ages now. Rage and bitterness and hate, unraveling like a spring. It's easier then to unzip the air-rifle slip, take out the gun, load it. He runs his hand along the wooden stock. Cool, comforting. It's on his side, a friend.

There's only the moonlight now to illuminate the yard. He stands up, rests the barrel on top of the stone wall, lines up the sights to bring the stone figure into focus, the girl-woman turning into fish.

He's got total concentration. That adrenalin hit. His mind's going blank.

The first shot he fires almost deafens him. He feels the whoosh of air, hears a muffled *crack* as the pellet hits stone. A trickle of dust. The pellet seems merely to have lodged itself in the stone. He loads again, fires, hits the hand. And again. He must be pitting the stone with holes, but nothing's breaking. There's no shattering into pieces like he'd hoped. The slingshot would have done a better job than this.

Leah and Matt Davies must have the music turned up loud enough to drown out the shots. Or they're busy with something else . . . with each other. The door's still firmly shut.

He loads again, aims, shoots. The head this time.

Shoosh shoosh. The sound pushes through the blankness in his head.

He tenses up, listens. Something else is moving out there in the mist and the dark. Brushing through the wet grass. A fox, perhaps, going about its own business.

He'd never shoot a fox. Something about the way they are: the sharp, intelligent eyes, their wildness. Hunters and scavengers. Survivors.

He freezes. Listens. He can't see anything; it's too dark and the sea mist has moved in closer over the field. It's much thicker now. He keeps one hand on the air rifle. The hair along his neck bristles like a hunted animal's.

He loads the air rifle again. Fires.

Light suddenly floods the yard as the back door swings open. Matt Davies swears loudly, stumbles towards the sculpture. "What the—?"

"What's going on? What's that noise?" Leah's voice.

But it's as if something's jammed in Simon's brain. He can't process the new information. His hand keeps loading, lining up, firing. He can't seem to see that it's not the stone figure that he's firing at any more, but the real thing, a person.

Leah shrieks out with pain. Matt Davies yells. There's the smash of splintering glass on stone.

The new sounds shatter something in Simon's brain. They drag him back from wherever he went, from that dark terrifying place where there are no thoughts and no feelings.

The yard is full of Leah's screams. Simon shrinks back in horror. *What have I done?*

He crumples down into the ditch at the base of the wall, shaking in sudden terror. He must have hit her. Matt Davies is swearing, calling out into the darkness. "What the hell do you think you're doing? Who is it out there? I'm calling the police—"

How bad is it?

He can't see a thing. He can hear Matt's footsteps on the path, the crunch of glass. *I must have hit the greenhouse too.*

"Who is it out there?"

Any minute now and Mr. Davies will look over the wall and find him, flush him out from his hiding place, and Simon's world will blow apart. He cowers, waiting, trembling all over, stifling sobs that rise and stick in his throat until he's almost retching into the ditch.

Leah's moaning. "My leg. Matt, my leg!"

All that noise means nobody is dead. Nobody dead. He repeats it like a mantra.

Matt's footsteps retreat from the wall. The voices go quieter. Leah is crying softly, Matt seems to be checking her out, calming her down. "Where? Show me. You'll be OK. It's OK. Let's get you inside—I have to see who's out there—and get my phone—"

"What if they shoot again? You'll be killed! Don't leave me by myself!" Leah's sobbing more quietly, but she's obviously terrified. Who does she imagine is out there?

Should he come out, own up? Explain it was all a stupid mistake, he never meant any of it . . .

But he can't. Can't move. Can hardly breathe.

He hears the brushing noise again, the footsteps in wet grass. They come closer and closer, until they stop right behind the place where he's half hidden in the long grass of the ditch. It's not a fox going about its own business. It's a man. And now he's so close, Simon could touch his foot. The battered leather of an old army boot. Next to the boot is the barrel of a shotgun, pointing downwards.

Of course.

Now it seems almost inevitable. Stupid not to have thought of it before.

Mad Ed.

Mad Ed's tall enough for Mr. Davies to be able to see him over the wall, even in the dark. Simon holds his breath, heart thudding. The barrel of the shotgun is horribly close to his head.

Matt Davies's voice rings out over the yard, clear and deadly calm. "So it's you. Shooting into my garden, hell-bent on ruining my work. And nearly killing a young woman while you're at it."

Simon hears his footsteps come closer to the wall.

"What the hell do you think you're doing? Are you crazy? You could've killed her with that bloody gun. Or me. Is that what you wanted?"

"It's that crazy man!" Leah sobs. "He's a bloody nut! Call the police! He's going to kill you!" She's getting hysterical again, crying so much Simon can hardly make out what she's saying. He hears the words "pervert" and "stalker."

"Get away from here!" Matt says. "Don't let me ever see you anywhere near here again. And lock that bloody gun up. You haven't heard the end of this. I'm calling the police right now."

The door bangs shut. The garden goes dark, then almost immediately the door opens again and light floods the yard. Simon hears footsteps, the slam of two car doors, the engine stuttering into life. The car moves slowly away up the track.

He must be driving her home. Or to the hospital. How badly is she hurt?

The cold and damp have seeped right through Simon's clothes to his skin. He's stiff and cold from lying cramped up, his arms around his body, in the narrow ditch. He lies there, straining for sounds.

Silence.

Now what? He is lying in a ditch in the dark, and just beside him is a madman. A madman with a gun, who for his own twisted, muddled reasons, has just taken the blame for the terrible thing Simon's done, without saying a single word in his own defense. What the hell's he going to do now?

What's even worse, absolutely no one else knows that Simon is here.

27

The feet shuffle a little farther away.

Simon makes himself open his eyes. Mad Ed seems to tower over him as he cowers in the ditch. He's holding the shotgun in one hand, muzzle down. Is this it, then? The place where all this has been leading?

Perhaps if Simon looks him in the eye it will help Mad Ed see who he really is. Simon. Only a boy. Not a soldier, or an enemy sniper, or even a fox.

Mad Ed in the farmhouse kitchen. The photograph. Two young men in khaki.

Not his brother, either.

Mad Ed's eyes look empty. Then they seem to focus for a moment, as if seeing Simon again.

I should say something, Simon thinks. *Thank him, even, for taking the blame.* But his mouth is dried up. He can't do it.

Mad Ed turns away abruptly, starts shambling away toward the cliff, his feet brushing through the wet grass leaving a silver trail. The darkness and mist swallow him up.

Simon lies in the ditch, shaking all over, for a long, long time. He can hear a strange muffled whimpering sound. It takes him ages to realize it's coming from himself.

When he's sure it's completely quiet, he crawls out. He's so cold and stiff from being curled up without moving for so long he nearly keels over. He rubs his legs, feels the blood begin to flow back. When he's eased up enough, he creeps back along the wall, up the track, and retrieves his bike from the hedge.

All the way home, mostly downhill, fast on the bike, he tries to make sense of what's just happened. Why didn't Mad Ed say anything, if he thought in his crazy way that Simon was his brother? And if it wasn't like that, if he knew all along it was Simon, why would he protect him like that, and not say anything afterwards? What the hell's going on? How come he knew Simon was there? Is he watching him all the time now? Watching his house? Watching and following.

Simon thinks again about the lost slingshot and the circle of stones, when they were camping that night. The heart of stones, on the rope cliff when he and Leah were there. His camping stuff, saved from Rick and his friend. The oyster shells.

All those times Simon's glimpsed him, just at the edge of his vision, always just moving off, away. The loner, the wild man, the headcase. And something more sinister: the madman for whom the fighting has never stopped.

And then that time at the farmhouse, when he saw something more. The muddle and the sadness, the photograph, and the wounded bird. And something else too close to himself to even think about . . .

He bikes on. He has to slow down; the mist is thicker

here, rolling in over the fields either side of the road.

Maybe, he thinks, *maybe I've had it all totally the wrong way round. Maybe, just maybe, he's never been dangerous at all. What if he's been watching out for me, trying to keep me safe all along? In his own, crazy way . . . And the stones, the shells, were not warnings, but gifts, offerings. . . . He stopped Rick, didn't he?*

He starts to think what will happen when the police arrive. They'll probably wait till morning; there won't be anyone manning the local police station till nine. And they'll start with questions and then they'll look for evidence, and at some point someone will realize that Leah's leg and Matt Davies's stone sculpture have not been shot with Mad Ed's shotgun after all, but with an air rifle. It won't take much to work out the difference.

It floods Simon with panic all over again. How can he possibly take the air rifle home now? It'll destroy his mother completely if all this comes out. Supposing Leah is really badly injured? He'll have to hide it somewhere. Chuck it over the cliff. Bury it. Something.

It comes to him in a flash of inspiration. The burial chamber. It's so deep and dark and out of the way, no one will find it there. And even if they do, they'll think it was Mad Ed who hid it there all along. Matt Davies won't have seen the gun in Mad Ed's hand, behind the wall, will he? It might just as easily have been an air rifle. Months later, when all this has blown over, when everyone's forgotten, Simon can go back and find it again and everything will be all right.

He cuts down the track he took ages ago, when he first found the Coffin Path. He leaves the bike at the stile and crosses the field on foot, then cuts across to the cliff. It's hard to find his way in the thick fog. The rifle feels heavy on his back, and getting heavier all the time. It must be really late. He's exhausted. He thinks he hears a car back on the road he's come off, but the sound is muffled. He hears the foghorn from the lighthouse. No light. The moon's disappeared.

He moves slowly now; the air changes. He might be near the cliff edge. You'd never see in these conditions. The sensible thing would be to stop right now, stay in one place, wait for the fog to lift or for daylight to dawn.

Now he can see something dark within the darkness. He edges forward, hands outstretched. He feels the living, breathing stone, the guard stones at the entrance of the chamber, rough against his palms. He takes a deep breath and plunges in.

His ears are ringing. He puts his hands over them. They feel cold, but the air in the chamber seems warm. When he takes his hands away he hears another sound, like a deep sigh. He can see nothing.

Deep breath. Don't think.

He edges forward. It's hard to know where the ceiling is; twice he bangs his head. He ends up dropping to his knees and crawling, one hand pushing out ahead so he doesn't hit anything. Bit by bit he feels his way through the series of chambers, deeper into the earth, it feels like. When he's as far back as he can go, with bare rock ahead and on both sides, a space only just big enough for his body, he feels along the rock, searching for a crack or a fault line or a gap between stones where he can shove the air rifle. And it's there, waiting: a smallish gap, just above his head, and he carefully takes off the gun and slides it into the space. It nestles there, safe. He can find it again, when the time is right. And so he edges back and finds a space big enough to turn his body, and then crawls back the way he came, feeling his way slowly, breathing deeply, focused entirely on his own movement. *Don't think. Don't think.*

He inches towards the grey light which must be sky. His hand touches something hard and cold; he flinches, then lets his fingers find the shape: a bracelet? Leah's, of course! She lost it here when . . .

Leah, who he has just shot.

He almost crumples.

No, keep crawling towards the light.

He makes himself do it.

He shoves the silver bracelet deep in his pocket and crawls forward.

A strip of light shines under Nina's door. Still awake, then. He tiptoes past.

"Simon?"

Oh no! She's heard him.

She opens the door. She looks awful.

"Where on earth have you been? It's so late, Simon. I can't go on like this, not knowing where you are half the time. You're only fourteen, for heaven's sake."

"Sorry."

"I missed you tonight. Feeling a bit lonely."

Simon stares at his muddy feet.

"Matt's a bit preoccupied. His new stone carving. His new model." She gives a wry, sad smile.

"She's much too young for him," Simon blurts out.

"You're much better than her!"

"Oh, Si!" She gives a little sob.

He lets her hug him, briefly. She feels soft and small.

"You're wet through!" she says. "What have you been doing?"

"I went in the fields," Simon says. "I went to look at the burial chamber in the moonlight. Only, the mist came down."

"It's not safe," she says under her breath. "The mist, the cliffs . . ."

"I know," he says, almost in tears. "But I'm here now, and safe, aren't I?"

He lies awake for ages. His body is damp with sweat. The window rattles. The wind's up. It will blow away the mist by morning. Far out in the Atlantic, huge waves will be whipping up, starting the long roll in toward the shore.

28

The stone in his belly has gotten heavier. His headache's worse. In the morning, Nina takes him down to the Surfing Shack to get his new wetsuit, and he has to pretend to be really pleased—it's her peace offering to him, after all. He is pleased really, but there's a shadow over everything now. He can't stop thinking about last night.

He dozes all afternoon while Nina and Ellie go over to Matt's house.

She's full of the news when she gets back. It's unbearable, pretending to know nothing, feigning interest, surprise. Covering his own tracks.

"Didn't Leah say that man had followed her once?" Nina asks him. "And he's been hanging around when you and the boys are in the fields, hasn't he? Perhaps we ought to tell the police about that too?"

"No." Simon feels the sweat beading along his hairline. "I mean, it's like you said—he's a bit weird, a loner, but he doesn't mean any harm."

"Simon! How can you say that now? Look at poor Leah. She's got a great big gash in her leg! And what he's got against Matt's sculpture I can't imagine! But I suppose that's the point—it's not a rational, thought-out thing. When I think of you wandering out on those cliffs—with him out there—last night even! Well, not any longer."

"What do you mean?"

"The police are after him now. Leah and Matt can press charges. . . . There's a history too, of other things. Police record. There are lots of rumors . . . not that I like to listen to that sort of gossip. Anyway, until they've got him, you take care, OK? No going off by yourself. Have you seen Leah yet?"

"No," Simon says.

"You haven't fallen out, you two?"

"Shut up, Mum. It's not like that. Stop looking at me like that!"

Secrets. Lies. Growing up.

He wishes there was someone he could tell about what really happened, up at Matt's place. What he did. But there's no one. How can he possibly own up now? What would happen to him? And to his mother. It would ruin everything for her. And now someone else is in serious trouble, and it's all his fault. And each hour he doesn't tell, it gets worse.

The wind keeps blowing all day and all evening. The weather is changing. Huge storm clouds are building out at sea. It'll be raining by morning.

The knot of fear in his stomach gets tighter.

He feels like he's waiting for something. In suspended animation.

He offers to babysit Ellie so Nina can go out with Matt Davies. He still hasn't seen Leah.

Over and over he thinks about what he did. Shooting

for real. What it felt like. How easy it was to lose it completely, become a sort of machine. It's terrifying. He could have killed someone.

Should he just go straight to the police and own up to what really happened? Whatever the consequences? So that Mad Ed doesn't get into deeper trouble?

Leah, he realizes, is the one person who knows about his air rifle. But she also knows that it's a secret, that Nina mustn't find out. There's no reason for her to make any connection between him and the shooting. Not when she saw Mad Ed right there with her own eyes. Is there?

He reads Ellie her bedtime story. She's moved on from the selkie story now, to one about a pioneer family living in the big woods. There's a description of a pig being butchered which makes Ellie squeal and cover her ears. When she's fallen asleep, he finds himself reading on, even though it's a children's book. It's strangely comforting.

He has a bath. He spends ages in there, submerged almost completely. He practices holding his breath underwater. He can do over a minute.

When he goes down to the kitchen to find something to eat, he hears the first squall of heavy rain hitting the window.

He switches on the TV. The local news comes on at ten twenty. There's something about a missing person.

Much later, lying in bed, he hears snatches of the shipping forecast from the radio in Nina's room. "Storm force eight, rising, heavy rain; visibility poor."

Tomorrow I'll go and see Leah.

That night, he dreams he's climbing the tall black stack just off the cliff, higher and higher, and it's raining, and his foot slips, and he starts to fall. He keeps on falling, down, down toward the deep black sea. It's so far, he wakes up before he hits the water.

Lying awake in the darkness, he listens to the rain and wind buffeting the house. He imagines the sea crashing against the cliffs. He imagines a huge tidal wave rising up and engulfing the whole spit of land that makes up this place, this almost-an-island.

29

The weight is still in his belly when he wakes up the next morning, and all through the next day, getting worse. He can't eat.

"You're coming down with something," Nina says. "I can tell."

He longs to lay his head in her lap and tell her what happened, like he'd tell her things when he was a small boy, and she'd stroke his hair and make everything better again.

That's all over now.

A police car draws up outside Leah's house. A man and a woman get out. Simon watches Leah's door open to let them in. She can stand, then. Walk around. Not badly hurt. Nina joins him at the window. He flinches when she strokes his arm.

"Why don't you go over and see how she is? When the police have gone. Don't be mad with her over Matt Davies, Simon. There isn't anything going on between them, you know. A mild flirtation, that's all. I asked him."

He hunches his shoulders, digs his hands deeper in his jeans pockets. His fingers brush against the cool metal of

Leah's bracelet.

"Look!" Ellie thrusts a card in front of him. "For Leah. I made it." It's all vivid felt-tip colors, a jazzy mess. "It's a picture of her," Ellie says.

Simon almost smiles. *Yes*, he thinks, *that's Leah*.

Ellie goes with him over the road. It's easier, having Ellie there. Leah looks pleased to see them. It's the first time, he realizes, that he's been inside Leah's house. It's weird, the way it's the same as theirs, but completely different because of the heavy old furniture, the swirly carpets. Ellie runs around, opening doors and poking into things.

Simon sits on the edge of a chair in the sitting room opposite Leah, who has stretched herself out on the sofa with her leg propped up on a cushion. *This is impossible*, he thinks.

Ellie runs back in and stands right in front of Leah. "Where's your mum?" she asks Leah. "Who's looking after you?"

"No one!" Leah laughs. "I look after myself. My mum's in a sort of hospital."

"Is she sick?"

"Getting better. She'll be home soon."

"You were in the hospital," Ellie says.

"Yes, but not to stay. Just so they could bandage my leg up properly. Lovely card, Ellie, thank you! Put it on the mantelpiece for me."

There's a vase of flowers there already, with a florist's card. Simon recognizes the handwriting. Art teacher italics.

Ellie sits down next to Leah and strokes her foot. "Does your leg hurt?"

"Yes, but not as much as it did."

"What did the police want?" Simon asks.

"Just had to go over what happened again," Leah says. "The man—Mad Ed—they can't find him. He's disappeared. No one's seen him."

Simon's heart is thudding wildly again. He feels sick.

Leah's giving him a funny look.

What does she know? Can she tell how agitated he is?

Ellie gets up again and fidgets with the row of china birds on the shelf above the fireplace. Then she sits on her hands, watching him and Leah.

Silence.

He keeps glancing at her leg. It's bandaged from the knee down. She's wearing that short denim skirt. And her turquoise top, and her hair twisted like a rope over one shoulder.

"I saw you with Nina yesterday," Leah says. "Got your new wetsuit, then."

"Yes."

"So you're going to do that surfing school?"

"Yes."

"Lucky you. Wish I could. Not with this leg, though."

"How do they know it was him?" Simon blurts out.

"Mad Ed? We saw him! Right by the wall."

"What if . . . what if he just happened to be there, but it was really someone else?"

Leah laughs. "Don't be ridiculous! Like who?"

For a wild moment Simon thinks he's going to tell her. But Ellie comes and leans against his legs. "Can we go now?" she wheedles. The moment's gone.

"You can go whenever you want," he tells her. "It's only

across the road."

"Thanks for your card, Ellie," Leah says.

Simon stands up. "I'd better go too."

"I won't be able to walk anywhere for a while," Leah says.

"No. I'm sorry."

"Are you?"

"About your leg. And everything."

"It's not your fault," Leah says.

He looks directly at her for the first time. Does she speak in all innocence? Or has she begun to work it out? Is she waiting for him to tell her the real truth?

He can't tell from looking at her face.

"Can't you stay a bit longer?" she says.

He sits back down. The room seems bare and empty. There are no books, he realizes. There's a magazine on the floor, and what looks like a college prospectus.

"What's that for?" he asks her. "You going to college, then?"

Leah shrugs. "I might. Your mother brought it over."

"It's good, what you said about your mother getting better," Simon says.

"Well, we'll see."

He tries to imagine what it's like for Leah, living here. All she doesn't have.

"Do you want me to make you a drink or a sandwich or something?"

She smiles then. "Nah, not hungry. But thanks, Si. Nina said she'd bring me some supper tonight."

"It'll be better soon, won't it? Your leg?"

"Yes. A week or two, maybe? That's when the GCSE results will be out too. Not that I care about them."

The silence in the room makes him feel dizzy. He can't think what to say.

Leah speaks again. "Then I'll be able to swim again. You can show me how to surf."

Simon stands up. "Better go," he says. His hand brushes against the silver bracelet in his pocket. He fishes it out. "I found this." He holds it out on the palm of his hand.

Leah squeals. "You clever thing! Where was it?"

"In the burial chamber," he says. His cheeks are burning.

"You went back there? Thank you, Simon!"

He looks at her face. Her eyes are shining, her cheeks have gone bright pink. So she does remember!

He places the bracelet next to her on the sofa and watches her pick it up, kiss it.

He knows that she means the kiss is for him.

She wouldn't, would she, if she knew what he'd really done?

He feels sick all day.

Simon watches the news while he picks at a plate of pasta that Nina insists he tries to eat. There's something about a new kind of bomb some American has invented, that kills people without damaging property. Next it's about a new manned space mission. Some government person talks about zero tolerance for youth crime. Another one goes on about lower standards in public-school examinations. Nina makes her usual comment about there never being any good news. She goes back out to the kitchen.

"Listen for what they say about the weather, Si," she calls out to him. "After the local news."

"A body has washed up . . . a man, drowned . . . possibly someone who'd fallen from the cliffs . . . so far unidentified . . ."

Simon's heart flutters wildly.

Mesmerized, he watches the reporter talking into the microphone against the familiar backdrop of the harbor wall and the town beach. Simon realizes it's exactly the news he's been dreading and expecting to hear, for days. The horrible news that lets him off the hook and condemns him to secrecy at the same time. It's him, isn't it?

It's Mad Ed.

By the next day the news has gone all over town and everyone knows who the drowned man is, and everyone knows why. It's the same man "wanted by the police for questioning about an incident at the studio . . ." For the first time, Simon finds out his real name: Edward Morvah, thirty-five, single, farm laborer . . .

30

It's early morning. No one else is up. Simon slips out of the house, walks purposefully down the road, turns left along the lane, past the last house with its wooden verandah and its view of the sea, climbs the overgrown stile into the tunnel of trees. He cuts himself a long straight hazel stick with the knife he inherited from his dad, peels the bark off as he walks slowly to the next stile.

He walks the Coffin Path across the fields, parallel with the sea for a while, climbing each stile without stopping to rest. Each stile is broad enough to rest a coffin: it takes at least six men to bear the weight of a dead man in a wooden coffin, and it's a long way across the fields to the churchyard. He imagines them, the six men, heaving the weight onto their shoulders for the next stretch of the path, sweating with the strain of it. But it's something to do for the dead man, isn't it? A last act of friendship, to carry him to his resting place.

He keeps walking until he's almost at Matt Davies's studio, and then he cuts across to the cliff edge and stands there.

The sea is slate grey today, whipped up with white

horses. Waves crash and boom on the rocks below, sending fine spume and spray up the cliff, over the grass, over him.

He thinks about Edward Morvah.

He tries to imagine what he was thinking that night.

Somehow he must have seen Simon, with the air rifle strapped to his bike, biking up the main road toward Mr. Davies's house. Followed him, just because that's what he always did. For his own muddled reasons.

And then he'd watched Simon get out the air rifle, rest it on the wall, aim it into the yard. Hovered, watching, waiting, not knowing what to do, and then he'd heard Matt and Leah come out, but too late to stop Simon from shooting . . . and so he'd taken the blame on himself to protect Simon, whom he'd muddled in his head with his own brother. Or maybe even with himself, the boy he'd once been, before things had gone so wrong for him. Or perhaps it was for some other reason, some strange, twisted logic that even Simon can't imagine. . . .

And then . . .

Hard to imagine the next bit.

Maybe he knew what the police would do, the way the story would sound, the other stories people round here would tell about a crazy man with a gun, living half wild on the edge of things, watching other people's lives: "Stalker . . . pervert . . ." Mad, or bad, or dangerous. All three, perhaps. And so he'd made his decision. . . .

Or maybe it wasn't like that at all. Perhaps it was just another accident. A step too far in the wrong direction. Easy enough to make a mistake in that kind of thick sea mist in the dark.

It isn't my fault, Simon tells himself over and over, *is it?*

People do their own crazy things. There are things you can't know, can't understand.

A darkness at the heart of it all.

He picks out five stones, slingshot-size. He hurls them out over the cliff edge, waits to hear the splash, but it never comes. The air has swallowed them up.

You could let something like this cast its shadow over your whole life. Or you could choose to see it another way: that it had been a simple act of kindness, one lonely man trying to stop a boy from suffering the consequences of a stupid mistake. You could accept it as meant, be grateful and move on.

There is always that choice; the dark or the light. Simon knows that.

He keeps on walking the Coffin Path, all the way to the cluster of stone buildings that make up the next village. A small church nestles in a dip in the land, surrounded by trees which have been blown almost horizontal by the wind off the Atlantic. They look like arms reaching out. Within the stone boundary wall there are gravestones and stone crosses, urns and angels, and the small mounds of earth which are unmarked graves. Simon picks his way between them, reading the inscriptions. "Lost at sea." "Reunited at last." "At rest." "Sleeping." "Dearly missed." "Never forgotten." He wishes they'd had a grave like this for his dad, a real place where he could go and talk to him sometimes. Tell him things. He can't remember the day they scattered his ashes all those years ago, even though Nina speaks about it sometimes. What he does remember is that he couldn't believe that was all there was left. Dust and ashes.

He thinks about that other burial place a few miles back: the stone burial mound made more than five thousand years ago by people living out here, on this far-flung fist of land surrounded on three sides by sea. Five thousand years of people being born, and growing up, and dying; the messy business of being alive. He thinks about his gun hidden deep in the deepest chamber, like all the other secrets swallowed up in its darkness.

He thinks about the things that can be buried, and the things that can't.

Simon goes home the coast-path way. The sea sends clouds of spume over the cliff edge. The rollers are magnificent. The wind tosses the gulls and kittiwakes and storm petrels like froth, and their cries are lost in the thunder of waves on the rocks below. It's the first big storm since they moved. He'll go surfing this afternoon.

About the Author

Julia Green has published several novels in her home country of Great Britain. *Hunter's Heart* is her first book to be published in the United States. The mother of two, Ms. Green also teaches writing to teens and adults. She lives in Bath, England.